CULLEN'S QUEST

Among the travellers on the stage from Stockton to El Paso were Robinson, a newspaperman who talked too much, and Hyde, who wore two guns and didn't talk much at all. Then there was Cullen, a salesman of ladies' underclothes. Most of them were concerned about the Comanche warrior, Black Dog, who was out on the warpath. But how had the Indian got so many new guns? And why should Cullen know so much about the West? Before these questions could be answered, lead would fly.

Books by Gillian F. Taylor
in the Linford Western Library:

DARROW'S LAW

GILLIAN F. TAYLOR

◆

CULLEN'S QUEST

Complete and Unabridged

LINFORD
Leicester

999 by

London

First Linford Edition
published 2001
by arrangement with
Robert Hale Limited
London

The moral right of the author
has been asserted

British Library CIP Data

Taylor, Gillian F.
    Cullen's quest.—Large print ed.—
Linford western library
1. Western stories
2. Large type books
I. Title
823.9'14 [F]

ISBN 0–7089–5925–3

Published by
F. A. Thorpe (Publishing)
Anstey, Leicestershire

Set by Words & Graphics Ltd.
Anstey, Leicestershire
Printed and bound in Great Britain by
T. J. International Ltd., Padstow, Cornwall

This book is printed on acid-free paper

Dedicated to the four who shared
the adventure:
Adam, Phil, Rory and Hugh.

Prologue

Baccy John had lived out in the Indian country for years. He had fought and traded with Comanches, Kiowa, Navajo, Pawnee, Tejas and Wacos. As he stepped outside, he looked as old and weathered as the adobe way station he tended down near the Rio Grande. Although he had ridden scout all through the War between the States, that had ended some four years back, Baccy John would never have admitted it to anyone, but his eyes were no longer sharp and the spots of age were showing on the backs of his hands.

Stretching and cursing, he wandered stiffly into the fresh morning. The sky was still glowing with dawn as he made his way to the corral. This halt on the old Jackass Mail route would do for him now. He cooked for the coaches when they stopped, and looked after the teams of company horses. There was a coach, and company, every couple of days, but no need for town manners or clothes. Baccy John shoved a hand beneath his undershirt to scratch the matted hair on his chest. He could hear the stamp of hooves and the eager whicker of a hungry horse. But when he lifted his eyes, the buttes and crags of the Sierra Blancas were foggy and dim. Even the pecan and cypress trees that bordered the nearby creek were an indistinct mass of moving colour. Baccy John had no chance of seeing the Comanche braves hiding nearby.

The boldest rose to his feet and padded forwards, his moccasins making no sound on the dry earth. The old white man was heading for the corral gate. Another Comanche rose from cover in the *bosque* of trees where the trail crossed the creek. Like the first, he had a new repeating rifle, but made no attempt to use it. A coup counted with a hand weapon made a

2

much better tale to tell. The nearest Comanche lifted a hatchet from his belt. He glided steadily over the open ground, his eyes on the old white man. His friend was a few paces behind.

Baccy John was getting old, but he wasn't yet helpless. The team horses in the corral tended to push against the gate when he came out in the morning, all eager for fuss and the walk to the creek. They were there now as he approached, the little black gelding blowing through its nostrils at him as always. But the white-faced sorrel had its ears pointing another way. It was looking at someone else. The thoughts flashed through Baccy John's mind. Only yesterday, when the eastbound stage had stopped, had the driver warned him that the Comanches were on the move again. Baccy John whipped around, his hand diving to the old Colt by his side. For a moment he thought it was a false alarm; the coppery skin of the young Comanche, and his antelope-skin leggings blended in with the dun and buff tones of the scenery. Then the Comanche dived forward with a war scream.

Old Baccy John had heard the sound before. He didn't flinch, but raised the heavy Colt and fired at the onrushing figure. He took a step back at the heavy recoil as another scream sounded; this time, of a man in agony. Even with his left arm torn half away, the Comanche dived on his enemy. Baccy John could see well enough at this range. He used the gun to block the swinging hatchet, then the two men collided. They went over backwards. John landed heavily, but kept his wits. Rolling over, he managed to pin down the Comanche's right arm. He didn't even need to aim. The Colt bellowed once. The single shot tore the Indian open. The air reeked of black powder and blood. The Comanche writhed and screamed, pushing Baccy John away in his death throes. The old man glimpsed the second Comanche closing, but his reflexes were too slow now. He was still on the ground as the Comanche dived, swinging a long knife. It tore across Baccy John's face and throat. Warm blood spurted down his chest as he struggled to raise his arm and get a clear shot. Black powder smoke hung in the morning air.

The young Comanche landed rolling and was back on his feet in a flash. He grunted his coup cry as the knife went in again. This time he buried it firmly in the white man's neck. Baccy John choked and flailed, but he no longer had the strength to lift the heavy gun. It was snatched from his hand as he died.

1

'It's sweltering again today, yeah?' said the lanky young man to no one in particular. As he spoke, he smoothed down his hair, which shone with some patent preparation for making it tidy. He looked out of place there in Fort Stockton, deep in the Texas south-west. He wore town clothes, while his bony face was decorated with the latest style of side whiskers. His skin was reddish with newly acquired tan and he tended to squint every time the restless wind raised a puff of dirt. What made him stand out most to Western eyes, was his complete lack of weapons.

'Is it always this torrid in the summer?' he asked generally.

People bustled past, all busy getting the stage ready to leave on time. No one bothered to answer the young Easterner. Bags, tools and barrels were lifted up and stored inside the large-wheeled wagon. A plough was strapped along the side and a crate of squawking chickens was tied to the back. It all looked more like some emigrant wagon than the gleaming stagecoach usually featured in travel advertisements. More dust rose in flurries as the snorting, eager six-horse team was harnessed up. The Easterner backed away, brushing at his clothes.

Gazing around, the young man spotted another traveller waiting patiently nearby with his own horse. The young man bounded across and held out his hand.

'Greetings, sir. I'm Hulton F. Robinson, from the *Rhode Island Chronicle*. What's your name?'

The other man stared back through narrowed grey eyes. He seemed to think over the question a moment before answering.

'Hyde.'

Even Robinson's enthusiasm waned a little under Hyde's withering expression.

8

He backed off a little but continued to sneak looks at the other man as if trying to commit him to memory.

Hyde was tall enough, without being as awkwardly coltish as the younger man. A bright yellow neckerchief enlivened his plain, grey and black clothing. Robinson stared more openly at Hyde's gun belt and the two Army Colts with ivory grips. Hyde stood quietly aloof from the hurly-burly, every inch a man who was busy minding his own business. Robinson dared get close again.

'Why do you carry two pistols?' he asked. Another short silence.

'One for each hand.'

'Oh.' Turning away, Robinson missed the faint gleam of amusement in the other man's eyes. The newspaperman sauntered away to the far side of the wagon. Once out of sight, he took notebook and pencil from his jacket pocket and made swift notes in shorthand. He moved aside absently to let a young married couple board the wagon, but didn't look up until a voice yelled;

'All aboard that's comin'!'

Stuffing his things back in his pocket, Robinson hurried to the front of the wagon and hauled himself up on to the driver's box. Hyde saw him climb up uninvited, and winced. The driver turned and saw Robinson beside him. The two men stared at each other.

'Gee!' Robinson exclaimed impulsively. 'I'd sure wish I'd been able to bring a camera, yeah? My editor would admire to see a photograph of you. 'A real Western type', he'd call it.'

The description was accurate enough. Whiskers Spragg was a true frontiersman. He was skinny and grisled, with a straggling beard, as greying as the rest of his shaggy hair. Blue eyes shone from his lined, weather-beaten face. He wore patched black trousers and a Kiowa buckskin shirt with quilled beading over the shoulders. His moccasins too were beaded and embellished with tin wrappings on the long heel-fringes. A

Colt Dragoon hung from one side of his gun belt, balanced by a skinning knife on the other side. He reacted to Robinson's comment like a true Western stagecoach driver.

'Get the hell off of my seat!' he bellowed.

Robinson froze.

'Go on, git!' Spragg lifted his long whip, letting the lash uncoil. He spat black tobacco juice past the young man's left ear, just for good measure.

'I'd really like to talk to you, sir.' Robinson turned on his winning smile. 'I'm a newspaperman, yeah, travelling about the West to catch the flavour of the picturesque for my readership.'

'An' I'm the driver of this wagon. What I says goes. An' I say, get the hell off my seat, you damned dandy greenhorn.'

'All right. Yes, sir.' Robinson backed down.

By the time he reached the back of the wagon, he had made up his mind to befriend the driver properly before trying to get a ride on the box again. They had a three-day journey ahead; that would be time enough.

Whiskers Spragg swung his whip high in the air, cracking it above his horses' heads. 'Next stop, El Paso!' he bellowed. His team threw their weight into the harnesses, testing the leatherwork and stitching as they strained to get the wagon and its load moving. It was 8 a.m. exactly and Whiskers Spragg boasted on his time-keeping as a driver. It was time to be gone from Fort Stockton.

'Wait!' Another passenger hurried from the company building.

'Whoa! Damn you to hell.' Spragg pulled on the ribbons, balking his team.

The latecomer threw his bag into the back and scrambled up. Although on the paunchy side, he moved energetically enough. Almost before he had landed inside, Spragg yelled his team on again. The wagon jerked, making the seated passengers sway. The latecomer almost fell but kept his balance gracefully. He glanced about; the nearest empty seat was beside a well-dressed middle-aged man, but the latecomer ignored it.

'Excuse me,' he said, picking his way past Robinson and the married couple to take a seat next to the only black passenger. 'Mind if I sit here?'

'Why no, suh. Doan' mind me none.' The black man hitched himself aside, leaving plenty of room for the other.

'Much appreciated.' Stowing his valise under the seat, the latecomer sat down.

The wagon had a roof and sides of canvas. Most of the panels were down, to keep out dust and glaring sunshine, but the ones at front and back were up. Wooden benches were spaced across the box for seats, with yet more luggage stowed here and there. A canvas sack with the official stamp of the US Mails was right behind the box where Spragg sat. Six passengers travelled inside, while Robinson could see Hyde riding close behind on his liver chestnut horse.

'Sorry for making the delay,' said the latecomer, speaking loudly enough to be heard by Spragg as well as the passengers.

The driver merely spat accurately at a clump of long grass. 'Ace,' he muttered.

'I'm Pat Cullen,' the latecomer went on. 'Travelling salesman; ladies furbelows and frillies.' He winked saucily at the young woman sitting on the bench opposite.

She blushed prettily and almost winked back; her young husband stared at his shoes.

'Hulton F. Robinson; I'm a news-paperman.' The gangly man looked expectantly at the fresh-faced couple.

'Don Schmidt,' the fair man said quietly. 'Me an' Mary's going out to take up the farm her uncle left us, near El Paso.'

Their clothes were so simple and modest that they might have been mistaken for Quakers or some such, if Mary Schmidt's dress hadn't been made of a cheerful yellow calico. The deep bonnet almost hid her sweet face with its rosebud mouth and dark, gypsy eyes.

'That's marvellous,' said Robinson with his usual enthusiasm.

'Hasn't your uncle left you any tools with his farm?' Cullen inquired, nudging an axe stored under the seats. The salesman was wearing a brown town suit, a derby hat and good boots. Sparkling blue eyes enlivened an otherwise plain, good-natured face, which carried a light tan. His waist was well-padded, but something in those eyes suggested a toughness in his character.

'We don't know,' Don Schmidt answered in his quiet way. 'We sold up our little place back in Ohio and got new farm goods.'

'What about you?' Robinson turned to the black man.

Cullen's companion seemed surprised at being drawn into the conversation.

'Ah's Wilbur Jefferson,' he drawled. He was a sturdy young man with skin the colour of milk chocolate and a mellow, deep voice. His clothing was simple, and patched, but was clean as possible while travelling the dusty trails. 'Ah's goin' West to look fer work,' he added with a hint of pride.

'What kind?' Robinson asked.

'Most any kind o' labourin', suh,' Jefferson answered. 'Ah's real good wit' critters but I kin turn my han' to most kind of anythin'. Jus' so long as it done pays real money.' He showed uneven teeth in a white smile.

Robinson found the thick drawl difficult to understand, but he puzzled his way through. 'Were you formerly a slave?' he asked, feeling in his pocket for his notepad.

Jefferson nodded solemnly.

'That's swell! I mean . . . well . . . ' Robinson flushed. 'I never met a freedman before. I'd really like to talk to you about it sometime, for my paper, yeah? The reading public in

Woonsocket would be most interested to read about first-hand experiences under the old plantation system.'

'Mebbe. Sometime later.' Jefferson looked at the floor of the swaying wagon.

'Please think about it.' Letting the notepad stay in his pocket, Robinson turned to the last of the passengers in the wagon. 'Would you care to introduce yourself?'

'Jack Wybourn,' the middle-aged man answered stiffly.

'And what is your purpose in travelling to El Paso?'

'I'm meeting someone on business. I have interests there.'

'And what kind of business might that be, Mr Wybourn?' Cullen asked mildly. There was nothing mild in his gaze.

'My own.' Wybourn stared straight back. Although he wore a good black suit and white shirt, his face was lined and tanned. His hair was grey and fell in a fore-lock over his forehead, but his neatly groomed goatee was still dark. A Colt Navy in a comfortably worn holster hung at his side, half hidden by the suit jacket.

'Of course.' Cullen smiled suddenly. 'My 'pology for asking.'

He stretched and yawned, trying to arrange himself comfortably against the sacks piled behind him. His task was made more difficult by being seated opposite Robinson, whose long legs took up plenty of room. No one spoke for a couple of minutes. Wybourn lit a cigar, without asking Mrs Schmidt if she objected, and sat blowing the smoke over the tail-gate. Robinson passed some time by peering through the gap between the canvas curtains, but the angle made his neck ache. Turning his attention back to his fellow passengers, he saw Pat Cullen yawning again.

'Up late talking to the stationkeeper,' he explained.

'Did you hear anything interesting?'

Cullen hesitated a moment, glancing briefly at Mary Schmidt. 'He said he'd heard rumours about the Comanches. Just that they were out buffalo-hunting.'

Up on the wagon box, Whiskers Spragg spat a stream of tobacco. 'Them Comanch' ain't hunting no buffalo,' he said clearly. 'That heathern varmint Black Dog's been stirring up the young bucks. Got 'em to cussin' the white folks and paintin' fer war. He reckons as how he's gonna make white folks too skeered to set foot outta town.'

Mary Schmidt gasped quietly; her husband clung to her hand.

'Are the Comanche really as ruthless as the stories say?' Robinson moved forward beside Cullen so he could lean out on to the wagon box. The notepad was in his hands.

' 'Course they are, boy.' Spragg twisted in place, trusting his team to make their own way along this easy part of the trail. He held all three pairs of reins in his left hand, leaving his right free for the whip or the brake. 'I kin tell you things about the Comanch' as would leave your face whiter'n a nun's underdrawers.'

'I see.' Robinson instinctively noted down the colourful expression, though his attention was on the talk.

'Let's not talk about it,' Cullen said, mindful of Mary Schmidt's presence.

'The Comanche should be made to go back on the reservation,' Wybourn said suddenly. It was the first remark he had made of his own accord, and it drew everyone's attention.

'Why do you say that?' Robinson asked. He twisted round, awkwardly folding his long legs in the confined space.

'They're a menace!' Wybourn said. 'Savages. They cannot be trusted to keep a peace, but roam aimlessly over this great land, taking what they want, in any way they want.'

'Wouldn't you say there's room enough for all, yeah?' Robinson asked.

'The land should go to those with the energy to use and improve it. The Indians are no more than dangerous, wild animals.'

'Don't you believe that it's our Christian duty to try and improve them?' Mary Schmidt asked softly.

'Mission schools have done a lot of good,' Robinson said.

'If you folks want Indians, you're welcome to them,' Wybourn snorted, pointing with his cigar at the young man. 'Try putting a Comanche in a mission school and see what happens. This country needs to be opened up for Americans.'

'Which Americans?' Cullen asked dryly.

'White Americans.' Wybourn stated it as fact. He remembered Jefferson's quiet presence and added. 'Industrious Americans; civilized folk who know how to labour.'

'It'll take the whole Army to get the Comanche off their lands,' Cullen said. 'But only a few men will get the chance to take over that land.' He stared at Wybourn.

The businessman met his gaze. 'Like you said a moment ago, the Comanches aren't a comfortable subject for talk just now.'

Cullen nodded slowly. Then he smiled, the expression lightening his jovial face and wiping away the sharpness of his tone.

'We've got a pretty long journey ahead. I suggest a few games to while away the time,' he said.

'Cards?' Don Schmidt asked hopefully.

Cullen caught Mary Schmidt's expression, and shook his head. 'I guess Mrs Schmidt doesn't play, and it'd be downright rude to leave her out. How's about a spelling match, in teams?'

'Does anyone have a Webster's to check the answers?' Mary Schmidt asked.

Cullen grinned, his blue eyes sparkling cheerfully. 'I reckon we've got us a dictionary, right there.' He prodded Robinson's long legs.

'I'll be happy to oblige,' the young man answered. 'And I do have Webster's dictionary with me if you doubt my knowledge.'

'Robinson, I couldn't even remember all those long words you use, let alone spell any of them.'

With a few words, Cullen settled the game as himself and Jefferson against the Schmidts. He didn't ask Wybourn if he wanted to join in, and the businessman didn't offer. Wybourn's gaze kept returning to the cheerful salesman. He stroked his neat goatee and frowned, as if trying to dredge up some memory. After a few minutes of thought, he gave up and settled uncomfortably against the wagon upright.

Riding along behind, Hyde could hear most of the conversation. He was relaxed and still in the saddle, moving easily with the liver chestnut gelding. Although he listened, and silently made his own guesses at spelling the words given, his grey eyes were constantly alert. He had planned to ride along to El Paso on his own, but if Comanches were on the war path, it made sense to travel in company. Hyde had immense faith in his ability to use his Colts and his Yellowboy rifle, but he was essentially a man of common sense. As he rode, he knew that Whiskers Spragg was also watching the country with the eyes of a frontiersman. A life on the frontier was more use than any number of bullets.

* * *

'Noon halt,' Whiskers Spragg called. Behind him, Robinson took out his silver watch and checked. The wagon driver had called the time to the minute, without needing anything more than the sun to help. Robinson noted the fact in his book, then leaned forward to watch as the wagon turned.

Spragg spoke to his team as they worked, deftly manipulating all three pairs of reins.

'Easy there, Betty; ain't no need to rush. Get around, Raven. That's right now. Hold up there you slab-sided crowbait.'

The horses nearest the wagon took tiny steps, turning almost on the spot as the furthest pair circled. The three pairs were loosely hitched but under Spragg's guidance they moved as one unit. It took no time for the wagon to be parked on a spit of firmer dirt in the bottom of the draw.

'My word, it feels good to stand up and move again,' Mary Schmidt said as her husband helped her from the wagon. She expressed the uppermost feeling of all the passengers. They stumbled, blinking, into the brilliant sunshine after four hours in the cramped, dim and stuffy wagon.

Hyde halted his horse near to the creek and dismounted. Wilbur Jefferson happened to be standing nearby. The black man moved closer, raising his hand as if to take the horse's reins. Hyde automatically held them out for him. Hyde stopped first, confusion showing briefly on his face.

'I'm sorry,' he said. 'I didn't mean to . . . '

'Doan' trouble yo'self, suh,' Jefferson answered calmly, lowering his hand. 'I understand. It jest be habit, that's all.' Hyde nodded, and took the horse to the creek himself.

Robinson absently smoothed down his hair as he gazed about. It was an attractive spot, with cottonwoods to provide shade, a scattering of wild flowers for colour, and the welcome sound of water in the shallow creek. Seeing Spragg unharnessing the team, he went to offer his help.

'You reckons on as you kin handle my team?' Spragg asked, spitting tobacco at a clump of brush and missing. 'Bitch.'

'We do have horses back East,' Robinson retorted.

Spragg flashed a grin from the depths of his wiry beard. 'I heard tell it was all trains an' such. You kin water Lincoln for me.' He pointed to the grey horse.

The stagecoach driver unhitched the first pair in the team, watching Robinson the while. The young newspaperman managed well enough until the grey Lincoln plunged his head deep into the clear, fresh water, then lifted it and shook himself violently. Water sprayed all over Robinson, as Spragg laughed. While Robinson gasped and cursed, the grey horse plunged his head back into the creek and drank greedily. Robinson brushed at the water but the light coating of dust on his clothes had got wet, and was clinging.

Before long, the horses had been tethered to graze and the people were eating a cold meal washed down with Mary Schmidt's good, strong coffee.

'This is excellent food,' Robinson remarked, taking another bite of the pressed meat that Whiskers Spragg had produced. The Easterner was lying sprawled out like a new-born colt. His patent hair-oil was losing its effect and his thick brown hair was beginning to curl at the ends. 'What is it?'

'Pemmican,' Spragg mumbled around a mouthful.

'It taste better than the usual sort,' Cullen said. He was sitting neatly cross-legged. 'Is it Indian made?'

Spragg nodded. 'Comanche.'

'What goes into it?' Robinson asked eagerly.

The driver washed his mouthful down with coffee. 'Buffalo meat mostly, dried an' pounded good. All kinds o' berries an' nuts. Pecans, walnuts, plums, cherries. The squaws mix it up good with tallow an' store it. Sometimes they use dog meat,' he added casually, taking another bite.

Robinson coughed suddenly. Don Schmidt muttered something.

'Oh, my gosh,' his wife said. She covered her mouth with her hand.

Jefferson went on chewing, apparently unconcerned. Hyde grinned, revealing a sharklike smile. Wybourn shook his head slightly as he puffed on another cigar. It was Cullen who took pity on the shaken woman. Wiping the grin off his face, he leaned over. 'Don't mind that old goat,' he advised. 'He's joshing you all. Comanches don't eat dog meat.'

Don Schmidt swallowed noisily. 'They don't?'

'Some tribes do,' Spragg said, laughing to himself. 'But not the Comanche. Dog's kin to Coyote, an' Coyote's taboo.'

'Fascinating.' Robinson dashed quick notes in his book. 'That's just the type of information I want to know, yeah? My readers will adore such details of Indian life.' At that moment, he was ready to forgive Spragg for any number of practical jokes.

'If you spend long enough out West, you might see a wampus cat,' Cullen told him.

'What are they? Where do they live?' Robinson was ready to spring to his feet and start searching.

Cullen shared a glance with Spragg. Robinson was too excited to notice. 'They're pretty shy,' Cullen warned.

'Mighty shy,' Spragg agreed.

Hyde nodded, giving his agreement to the joke. Robinson looked around at the three of them, acknowledging them as the most range-wise of the party.

'Mighty purty little things, wampus cats,' Spragg went on.

'Are they likely to trouble farm stock?' Schmidt asked anxiously, earning himself a withering look from his wife.

'Not in the day,' Cullen said. His pleasant face was deadly earnest as he spoke. 'They sleep through the day, in low scrub like that.' He pointed a little way upstream.

Robinson looked thoughtful. 'I've not got much practice at moving quietly in the rough country. Do you think I might be able to find one sleeping?'

'You could certainly try,' Cullen said encouragingly.

'They mostly beds down under juniper,' Spragg added helpfully. 'I kin let you have ten minutes afore we needs to be goin' again.'

The young newspaperman jumped to his feet. 'I'll try,' he said resolutely. 'That's the best I can do.'

'Good for you.'

The group around the little fire watched as Robinson strode away to the undergrowth to look for an imaginary animal. Hyde rocked back and forth with silent laughter.

'That fool greenhorn couldn't sneak up on a deaf ol' Choctaw granmaw,' Spragg hooted.

Don Schmidt had caught on to the joke at last and looked disapproving. Wybourn merely looked bored. As they watched, the Easterner slowly crouched down and disappeared from view. They could see leaves shaking on the juniper bushes. Robinson was moving carefully, a couple of feet at a time. The bushes went still again. The people watching held their breath.

'Yeeoow!' Robinson burst free from the bushes, holding out his arm.

Something long dangled from his sleeve, thrashing madly in the air. The snake coiled and twisted and twisted itself into knots as it hung from his wrist.

2

Robinson blundered his way through the undergrowth, snapping branches as he ran.

'Help! Help!'

He shook his arm. The snake clung relentlessly, coiling and uncoiling. Robinson continued to run back to the others, still panicking.

'Goddam it!' Spragg exclaimed, reaching for the Dragoon Colt holstered at his side. He needn't have bothered.

Cullen barely saw the movement as Hyde snatched out his revolver and fired, all in one smooth motion. The writhing snake jerked, its head cut off by the single shot. It fell to the ground in two parts. The long body twitched briefly and stilled. Almost before anyone knew what had happened, Hyde had holstered his gun again.

'Help!' Robinson rushed up, holding out his arm. His face had gone white.

'Lemme see,' Whiskers Spragg took the young man's arm and pushed his sleeve up.

Hyde got up and went to look at the snake's body. 'It's cotton-mouth,' he called back, turning the head over with the toe of his boot.

Cullen shook his head anxiously. Even Wybourn had stopped puffing on his cigar and was watching with concern. Don Schmidt was mumbling something under his breath but his wife was with Spragg examining the wound. Robinson collapsed to his knees, trembling.

'Oh, God; a snake. I didn't see it there,' he moaned.

'I'm real sorry,' Cullen said.

'Don't need to be too sorry,' Spragg said. He held out Robinson's arm for the others to see. The faintest red mark could be seen on the underside of his wrist, along with a small damp patch on the cuff of his jacket. 'The snake bit plumb into his sleeve. That fancy town jacket just about saved your life, boy.'

Robinson gaped for a moment, then the news sank in. 'Oh.' He sat back, silent for once.

'That must be a miracle!' Jefferson exclaimed, a wide smile breaking on his dark face.

'I believe you are right,' Mary Schmidt agreed. Robinson just closed his eyes.

There was a brief silence, broken by Whiskers Spragg.

'I guess I'd better go get that team ready.' Cullen and Hyde went with him, the three sharing rueful glances.

'Damn fool greenhorn,' Spragg muttered, tearing off a lump of black chewing tobacco and popping it in his mouth. 'Shovin' his hand into holes like that.'

Hyde nodded. 'Even a kid'd know better,' he drawled.

'That was some fine shooting,' Cullen remarked, pausing beside him.

Hyde returned a bland look. 'Learned to shoot some during the War.'

'We all did, but not many got that good.'

'Just a talent. Comes in mighty handy now an' again.' Hyde's narrowed eyes were unrevealing.

'Sure.' Cullen nodded amiably, and went to catch up one of the team horses. His face was thoughtful.

The wagon had barely got under way again before Robinson recovered his usual enthusiasm for life. Taking out his notebook, he wrote rapidly, pausing now and again to chew the end of the pencil.

'This will make a marvellous subject for my next letter to the *Chronicle*,' he said.

'I'm real glad you didn't get hurt,' Cullen said.

Robinson gawped at him innocently. 'It wasn't your fault that there was a snake in the undergrowth. It could have bitten any of us who went that way, yeah?' Cullen merely nodded, unwilling to explain the deception.

Robinson wrote some more, asking what kind of snake it had been. A few moments later, he paused, pencil hovering in the air. Tucking his things away, he climbed to the back of the wagon, peering over the tailgate into the sunshine. Hyde was riding just a few feet away.

'Excuse me,' Robinson called. 'Mr Hyde?'

'Yes.'

'I want to thank you for that marvellous display of shooting. You may well have saved my life, yeah?'

'It was no trouble,' Hyde drawled, unembarrassed.

Robinson climbed on to the tail-gate so he could talk to the rider more comfortably. He had to cling on to the cover supports as the wagon bounced over the rough trail. There was obvious curiosity on his face, but he spoke more tactfully than before.

'Pardon my asking, but your skill with guns really is remarkable. Did you learn to shoot during the War between the States?'

'I learnt pistol shooting some time before then,' Hyde drawled. His voice was neutral, so Robinson ventured another remark.

'You have kept your skill up since. Do you practise much?'

Hyde took a little longer to answer. 'I find it comes in real useful sometimes.' His hands moved automatically on the reins as his horse reached to snatch a mouthful of leaves from a bush.

'I'm grateful for that,' Robinson said sincerely. 'I'm going to write about it for my paper, yeah? Do you object to my use of your name in the piece?'

'No.' Hyde suddenly flashed a smile of private amusement.

'Thank you.'

Robinson dithered a while longer, his mouth half-open as if wanting to ask another question. He frowned, as if working out what he wanted to say. Hyde gave him no encouragement. After a few moments, Robinson nodded and withdrew back into the shade of the wagon.

'The man is a shootist,' Wybourn stated.

Robinson blinked at him. 'You believe he makes his living from his guns?'

'Why else should a man carry two pistols?' Wybourn said. 'Most men would consider one to be adequate, even out on the frontier.'

Robinson looked at the other passengers, to see what they thought. The Schmidts were as uncertain as himself. Wilbur Jefferson shrugged, offering no opinion. Cullen nodded.

'It's possible,' the salesman said quietly. 'But he could be useful to know.'

It registered briefly as an odd comment but was forgotten almost immediately. A new idea had occurred to the newspaperman.

'Could he be an outlaw?' he asked in hushed tones. Mary Schmidt gasped and clutched her husband's hand.

Cullen laughed. 'He might, but then so might any of us be. I've got this,' he patted a shoulder holster hidden under his suit jacket. 'Wybourn there's got a Navy Colt I'm real sure he can use, and Spragg's got himself a Colt Dragoon you could blow a hole through an ironside with.'

Robinson thought for a moment. 'I'm not carrying anything larger than a penknife,' he said sincerely.

Cullen burst into merry laughter, provoking smiles from the other passengers. 'Mind you don't slit some-one's wrists with that toadsticker then.'

Robinson grinned self-consciously. 'I guess maybe I was getting over-excited there.'

'Reading too many newspapers addles the brain.'

'Pays a living wage, yeah?' Robinson countered. 'And it beats selling clothes.'

'I like women's underwear,' Cullen protested. 'Preferably with a pretty little woman still in them,' he added.

Mary Schmidt giggled, looking more

gypsyish than ever. Cullen leaned forward, whispering into her bonnet. 'I've got some samples your husband would sure admire to see you wear.' He withdrew, setting a look of studied innocence on his face.

Don Schmidt seemed about to say something when Whiskers Spragg brought the wagon to a sharp halt.

'Whoa up there,' he called to the team. 'Hold up there, my lovelies.'

Robinson climbed between Cullen and Jefferson to lean out on the box.

'What have we stopped for?' The question became a shout as the driver picked up his shotgun from its boot and jumped down. Cullen saw that Spragg had taken his gun, and kept his head safely inside the canvas wagon-covers. Robinson climbed right out on to the box for a better view.

The wagon driver had left the trail and was cautiously approaching two dead steers. Hyde had halted his horse a short distance away and drawn his Yellowboy rifle. He held it across his lap as he watched the landscape. A single dead steer was no cause for concern, but two so close together seemed odd. Whiskers Spragg didn't trust anything odd that happened in Indian country. He walked slowly across the dry ground, his moccasins noiseless. All the time his eyes were scanning for tracks. The only signs were those of the dead animals kicking up the ground, and some dried blood. The nearest steer was a brindled red beast, with a magnificent spread of curling horns. It had been shot half a dozen times. A quick glance showed that the other had died the same way. Kneeling down, Spragg used his skinning knife to dig into the stiff carcass. Fetching out a deformed bullet, he wiped his hand briefly on his patched trousers and returned to the wagon.

'What is it?' Robinson asked, climbing down. The other passengers climbed out, curious, and glad of the chance to stretch their legs.

Spragg held out the bullet. 'Them

42

cows was used for target practice.'

Wybourn took the piece of lead. 'Looks about right for a Winchester,' he said. 'It's not big enough to be a Spencer shell.' Cullen and Hyde agreed with him; both looked worried.

Robinson took the mangled bullet, bouncing it in his hand to guess the weight. 'Some stockman must have been trying out a new weapon,' he said.

Spragg shook his head. 'Not on good steers like them. Beef is about the only source of *dinero* down here. They ain't been butchered none either,' he added, spitting at a clump of gramma grass.

'Indians are the only ones who would shoot good cattle and then not bother butchering them,' Cullen explained. 'And a casual thief wouldn't waste more than one bullet on each cow.'

'Which means that Black Dog's men have done got hold of repeating rifles,' Hyde drawled.

Cullen didn't answer, preoccupied with his own thoughts.

Robinson slipped the bullet into his jacket pocket. 'We're not molesting the Comanche,' he said seriously. 'We're not moving on to their hunting grounds, so is it at all likely that they would attempt an attack on the stagecoach?' This sincere question was greeted by a stunned silence from the Westerners.

Whiskers Spragg was the first to find his voice. 'Sonny, some buck's gonna be mighty disappointed when he tries to earn hisself some glory by takin' your scalp. You's just too damn green to be any fight.' He spat at the gramma grass again and missed. 'Bitch.'

'I don't believe that all Indians are bad,' Robinson insisted.

'They're not,' Cullen agreed. 'But the younger men have to get on in the world somehow, and fighting is how they do it.'

'Can't the older men order them not to?' Don Schmidt asked, getting the question in before the newspaperman could.

'Not likely, especially among the Comanche.' Cullen looked at Spragg for confirmation.

The frontiersman nodded. ' 'Comanch' is individuals. The old man warriors get to say a lot about huntin' an' the like, but the young bucks don't have to listen to no one iffen they don't want to. An' iffen it's Black Dog's got repeating rifles, why then he's got himself a whole lot of medicine.'

Wybourn spoke up. 'I suggest we get under way again. The sooner we reach Lone Cottonwood, the better. When we get to El Paso, we can send a message to the Army. If Black Dog's men have repeaters, they must be brought under control and sent back to the old reservation.'

'Ace. I agrees with Wybourn there,' Spragg said. Without wasting more words, he climbed back on to the wagon box.

The passengers returned to their hard benches. Jefferson had kept quiet all through the talk about the Indians, but as he sat down again, he muttered darkly about the wooden seats. Cullen overheard the remark, and grinned at him.

'When I've done earned me some wages, I'm a-goin' ter buy me a silk cushion stuffed full with feathers,' Jefferson said with feeling. He rolled his eyes as Spragg cracked his whip over the heads of his team and set the wagon bouncing and jerking again. Hyde rode his horse further from the wagon, keeping his rifle ready across his lap as he scouted for danger. Wybourn rolled up one canvas curtain from each side. Robinson futilely brushed the extra dust from his clothes, but said nothing. He kept his eyes open too, squinting in the harsh sunlight as they rolled along the trail. Now and again he pressed his hand against the misshaped lead in his pocket; a solid reminder of reality out here.

★ ★ ★

As the afternoon wore on, with no further signs of Indian activity, Robinson, Jefferson and the Schmidts began to relax. The more experienced Westerners remained quietly uneasy. Cullen wedged himself against the sack of mail and dozed for an hour, snoring lightly now and again. Wybourn sat alone at the back, smoking slowly on his rich cigar. He spoke little, but glanced frequently at the range. Robinson got Don Schmidt to tell him all about the little farm back in Ohio that he had sold up before moving West. Mary interrupted now and again, mostly to ask Robinson about life back in New England, and the fashions there. Jefferson listened with interest but rarely intruded in the conversation. Robinson noticed, and asked a few questions about the crops farmed in the South.

He soon got the ex-slave and the Midwest farmer engaged in conversation about farming practice, and sat making notes. It wasn't, perhaps, relevant to his letters about life on the frontier, but he hated to miss getting good material of any kind. Having started a conversation, he sat quietly, and let the people around him talk. When Cullen woke again, his sharp eyes noted what was happening. He stayed propped against the mail sack and watched, his opinion of the young newspaperman rising.

When Lone Cottonwood staging-post finally came in sight, there was a sigh of relief all round. While halts on the main routes run by companies like Wells, Fargo were intended solely for a change of team and driver, this one was a night halt. Ted and Betty-Lou MacKenzie were both waiting under the canvas awning out front as Spragg halted the wagon.

'Come right on in, folks,' Betty-Lou encouraged warmly. 'There's good java in the pot right now, and I'll have you-all a good, hot meal fixed afore that ol' whiskery buffalo gets through with his hosses.'

'I'm plumb pleased to see you too, Betty-Lou,' Whiskers Spragg said, spitting at the solitary tree.

Betty-Lou ignored him and spoke to Mary instead. 'It's sure nice to see another woman now an' again. That's a real pretty dress you got on.'

'Thank you. Can I help you fix the food?' Mary asked, walking gratefully into the shade of the awning.

'Hell, no! You-all just rest some. There's water for you to wash up afore you eat.' Betty-Lou's attention wandered as she spoke, her gaze settling on Robinson.

The young man was standing before the adobe stage halt, walking here and there to see it from different angles as he made notes. Hyde was watering his horse at the nearby creek. Spragg and MacKenzie were unharnessing the team. Jefferson, Wybourn, Don Schmidt and Cullen had all gone inside to the welcome shade and coffee. Robinson had seen a few adobe buildings in his travels through

49

Texas, but never one quite like this. It wasn't white-washed, but stood plain and dun. It was turf-roofed, with grass and flowers growing freely on top. The awning was fashioned from faded and patched canvas that had once been a wagon cover, and was supported on rough-hewn poles. Where these had come from was a mystery, for the only tree visible was a solitary cottonwood, with a home-made rocking chair stationed in its shade. None of the narrow windows had glass, but shutters with blistered paint were hooked open. There was a large corral a short distance from the house, a smaller one for the Mackenzies' horses, a henhouse and a washing-line that stretched between the last two. A buckboard was parked beside the smaller corral. A few pink geraniums in tin cans adorned one window ledge in sophisticated contrast to the softer colours of the wild flowers growing on the roof. All this Robinson eagerly recorded.

Betty-Lou leaned closer to Mary and

whispered. 'Is he from the government?'

Mary laughed and explained about Robinson being a newspaperman from the East.

'Oh,' said Betty-Lou, smoothing down stray hairs from the long braid coiled on the back of her head.

For supper, the hungry travellers were given generous platefuls of chilli. After the first, careful taste, Robinson wolfed his down and asked Betty-Lou what it was made of. The Schmidts ate more carefully, sharing apprehensive glances with Jefferson; all three left food on their plates. Afterwards, Betty-Lou insisted on taking Mary aside into her bedroom for a good talk about women's things. This left the men free to amuse themselves.

'I suggest a few hands of poker.' Cullen produced a pack from his suit pocket. The other men agreed, apart from Jefferson, who excused himself.

'Ah don' have much money, an' I cain't be makin' out wit' less'n I got now,' he drawled.

51

'Lady Luck might smile on you, yeah?' Robinson pointed out, depositing a handful of coins and notes on the table in front of himself. 'You may come out ahead.'

Jefferson grinned. 'Ah ain't played poker none, suh. Ah reckons as Ah'll lose dat gold fer sure.' His wise eyes glanced around the more experienced players.

Cullen had offered the pack to Hyde, who examined them efficiently before nodding his satisfaction. Cullen took them back and shuffled them with the grace of long practice.

As they played, Cullen and Robinson kept up a general conversation. The salesman had an endless fund of funny stories and jokes, all told with his wry humour and a certain amount of slapstick. The others were largely content to listen to him, Hyde chuckling to himself and even Wybourn smiling now and again. Spragg interrupted from time to time, countering one tale with another. As the whiskey bottle went round, the tales got wilder. Spragg was soon boasting about the team out in the corral.

'Them's the finest team in Texas,' he told Robinson. The old man scratched at his straggly beard. 'Why, they once hauled three wagons hitched together.'

'Three?' Robinson fanned his cards out and rearranged them. Spragg nodded solemnly. 'Three. All packed with silver, too.'

'Who needed that much bullion transporting out here?' Robinson asked, as he pushed twenty cents into the pot. It wasn't much, but he had already lost most of his stake for the evening.

'The mines,' Spragg answered. He spat a stream of tobacco into the dented brass pot by the stove. 'There was goddamn silver mines in the mountains out by El Paso.'

'Are they still producing?' Don Schmidt asked with ill-concealed interest.

MacKenzie and Spragg both laughed. 'There be silver out there for sure,'

53

MacKenzie replied. 'Happen you don't mind the Comanch' liftin' your scalp whiles you're diggin' it.'

'I should love to view a silver mine,' Robinson said. He saw Wybourn's raise of another twenty cents.

'You won't have the chance unless the government do their duty and force the Comanches to return to their reservation,' Wybourn announced. He was sitting upright on the plain bench, puffing on another cigar. A shot glass stood in front of him, its contents almost untouched. He had taken his suit jacket off but otherwise looked almost as neat as he had that morning.

'Why are you so keen for the Comanche to be cleared off?' Cullen asked. 'You got shares in a silver mine out there?' His voice suggested a joke but his round face was bland.

Wybourn hesitated for the barest moment before answering. 'I'm no prospector. But I have shares in the El Paso bank. That is the limit of my interest in mining.' Cullen nodded and smiled, but the warmth didn't reach his eyes.

The hand was won by MacKenzie. He gathered in the coins scattered on the battered table, and picked up the cards to shuffle them. Don Schmidt stretched and yawned.

'I'd best not play any more,' the fair young man said. 'I'm pretty much out of money.'

Spragg grinned. 'Sure an' iffen I had me a pretty li'l prairie hen like yours, I'd be goin' to bed early too.'

'I had better refrain from further play too,' Robinson said, picking up the seventeen cents left in front of him. 'I don't mind losing some money for the entertainment of the game, but I'd rather spread my losses over several nights.'

'A wise practice,' Cullen agreed. While talking, he had been keeping a sharp eye on how the other men had played. Wybourn was disinclined to take chances, but had shown himself to be a ruthless bluffer, unwilling to make allowances for the inexperienced players. Spragg and MacKenzie had taken both winnings and losses evenly, enjoying the socializing while still coming out a little ahead. Hyde had played steadily, transferring cash to his pocket every time he got more than five dollars in front of him. He had never built the stakes high or grumbled at losing, but he definitely played for gain. Cullen made a mental note of the fact but said nothing.

'We got us a long ride tomorrow,' Spragg said. 'Reckon I'll git me some coffee an' turn in.'

Robinson looked around the room. 'Where do we sleep?' The two other rooms were already in use and he could only see a single rough bunk in this room.

'This is it, feller,' MacKenzie said as he rose. 'Plenty of room on the floor.'

'Then who gets the bed? Should we draw straws?'

'The cot's mine.' Spragg moved

with surprising speed to sit on the bunk. 'Driver allus gets the bunk.' He bounced on the thin mattress, which rustled.

'But we've paid passage.' Robinson looked around at the other men, but they were busy picking spots on the hard-packed dirt floor.

'An' I'm the driver. I'm doin' all the blasted work, so I get to sleep on the bunk. Company policy.'

'Here.' MacKenzie thrust a couple of tartan blankets into Robinson's arms. The young man noticed that they smelt faintly of horses. 'You aim to learn some about the West. Well you kin learn to sleep like the folks out here do.'

'Consider it an adventure,' advised Cullen, who had swiftly contrived himself a neat bedroll.

Robinson grunted, stared reproachfully at Whiskers Spragg and set about trying to arrange himself a bed. He wasn't best pleased to discover that the choicest spots had gone, and there wasn't anywhere for him to stretch his long legs out.

★ ★ ★

Spragg was the first to wake in the night, alerted by the sounds from the corral. The old frontiersman sat up, still wearing all his clothes except hat, gun belt and moccasins. He listened a few moments longer, then swung his legs off the bunk, cursing under his breath. The movement was enough to waken Hyde.

'Comanche?' he hissed, one hand already resting on the butt of his gun.

'Somethin's disturbed my hosses,' Spragg grunted quietly as he slipped on his moccasins. Still fastening the gun belt, he picked his way to the door.

Hyde could hear the sounds too. The horses were milling around in the corral, whickering excitedly and snorting. There was a chance that marauding wolves or even a puma had alarmed them. Pausing briefly for boots and gun belt, he followed the older man.

The night was lit only by the stars, blazing brilliantly in the black sky above the desert. Neither man spared them a glance, both being alert for trouble on the ground. Spragg glided towards the corral, his heavy old Colt Dragoon in his right hand. Hyde left him to see to the horses, moving out wider to scout.

The team horses were milling around, heads and tails high. The MacKenzies' two horses were alert too, both pressed against the poles of the smaller corral, but Spragg was only concerned for his own team. As the horses paused a moment from their wheeling, he heard other hoofbeats. They were the muffled sound of unshod horses coming closer.

Hyde heard them too. He froze, a gun ready in each hand. The night breeze blew steadily into his face as he waited. A few moments later he glimpsed dark, shadowy horses running closer through the night. The drumming grew louder before being drowned by the noise from the corrals. Hyde crouched, his weight on the balls of his feet. Everything was in shades of grey in the night. His own grey trousers and pale blue shirt toned in with the star shadows of the night. Even though he knew where Spragg was, the other man was an indistinct shape by the corral.

One of the team horses whinnied suddenly, rearing up and charging to the gate. Her panic was infectious. Horses milled around, bumping into each other in the enclosed space and crashing against the log walls. Hyde thumbed back the hammers of his revolvers and waited for the raiders to get just that little bit closer.

3

Inside the adobe others were waking too. Robinson disentangled himself from his blankets and hurried to the half-open door without bothering to put his shoes on. He paused there just long enough for Jefferson to grab the back of his shirt as he was about to slip through.

'Doan' be goin' out there, suh,' he hissed.

'I want to see . . . ' Robinson pulled himself away and leaned through one of the windows.

'I'm sure there be wild Indians out there,' Jefferson said. 'Yo' is gwine ter get yore head blowed clean off, suh.'

'He's talking sense,' whispered Cullen, who had taken up position by the door. The salesman had a short-barrelled revolver ready in his hand. In spite of his town suit and soft build, he looked like a man who knew what he was doing.

Robinson retracted himself a little, but couldn't help leaning his elbows on the window ledge as he peered hopefully out into the darkness.

★ ★ ★

Whiskers Spragg saw his beloved team horses crashing around inside the corral. He ran for the pole gate, anxious that one of them might trip in the confined space and fracture a leg. Hyde's chestnut was racing among the mob, but Spragg gave it little thought except as a hazard to his team. The heavy old Colt he shoved back into its holster. Reaching the corral, he took the lowest pole from its socket, letting it drop to the ground. As he worked, he called to the team, pitching his voice to carry over the thunder of hooves, without sounding anxious.

'Come on now, you dang fool hosses. Ain't no need for you to be acting plumb loco like this.'

One of the greys bumped against another horse and staggered away. It hopped over the rails and found itself outside the corral.

'Easy there now, Raven,' Spragg called.

The gelding threw up its head and snorted. It was almost white, and showed like a pale ghost in the starlight. Another horse jumped over the poles, almost colliding with the grey. The strange horses were bearing down on them now, raising fine dust across the yard, The bay mare snorted and burst into a gallop. Spragg pressed himself against the corral poles as the powerful horses wheeled together. Others from the corral had joined the loose horses. They squealed with excitement, milling together.

The strange horses were scrubby mustangs, like most Indian ponies. This close to them, smelling their sweat, Spragg could see that the loose ponies were unmounted. They didn't have so much as a woven-grass hackamore between them. One arched its neck and gave a trumpeting call.

'Goddam wild stallions!' Spragg yelled furiously.

The loose horses were a group of young bachelor stallions. They had smelt his team mares and come looking for them. Even as Spragg realized the truth, the mob of horses were racing away. MacKenzie's two, still in their little corral, called to the others. One reared, and ran to jump out, but stopped short.

'Goddam, blasted, cow-hocked, slab-sided, coffin-headed, no-good, fool, scrub stock!' Spragg bellowed after the racing herd, shaking his fist in the air.

Hyde had worked out what was happening too. Somewhere in the stampeding herd was Cob, his good liver chestnut. In the dark, the browns, bays and chestnuts were almost impossible to distinguish. Angry at seeing his horse loose, he expressed himself by firing shots into the air.

Spragg had climbed into the corral and had almost captured one of the two horses left inside. The shots caused the brown gelding to swing away and crash into the fence. The galloping horses picked up their pace.

'What in hell're you doing?' Spragg yelled. He stormed from the corral to remonstrate with Hyde.

'You let the horses loose,' Hyde snapped.

'Better'n seein' them sprainin' an' breakin' legs in there,' Spragg jerked a thumb in the direction of the corral.

'And now they've gotten loose! Is that any better?' Hyde's voice stung with sarcasm.

'It sure as hell is. Or it would be iffen you hadn't scared 'em all to hell an' back. My team'll find their ways back soon enough.'

'My horse was in that corral too.'

While Spragg gestured fiercely, Hyde stood stiff and still. The two men faced each other, oblivious to the curious audience they had drawn. Robinson, Wybourn and Jefferson had left the adobe house and were listening to the argument with great enjoyment.

'My money's on Spragg,' whispered Robinson.

'Ah ain' takin' no bet,' Jefferson answered, just as quiet.

With all the excitement, no one noticed that Cullen had not joined them. Back inside the adobe, he was kneeling beside Wybourn's bedroll. He worked swiftly, his attention switching between the door and the back rooms. One after another, he searched Wybourn's long boots. He felt the fine leather and even ran his fingers over the wooden heels, feeling for any kind of hidden pocket or slit. His pleasant face was tense, the normal good humour replaced by intense concentration. Cullen put the boots back exactly as he had found them and wasted no time in reaching for the black Stetson. Again he searched, running his fingers around the inside of the brim. This time he found a folded paper tucked inside the sweatband. Snatching it out, he replaced the hat and moved to the door.

There he unfolded the paper with shaking hands and peered at it in the faint starlight. It was a receipt from the Winchester Firearms Company, for thirty new repeating rifles and a hundred boxes of ammunition. Cullen's face fell as he read. He took a sharp breath, as if he wanted to scream, but stopped himself. A moment later his whole expression changed. Moving faster now, he refolded the paper and tucked it inside the waistband of his trousers. Cullen opened his own valise and searched quickly for some paper. He found an old receipt about the same size as Wybourn's and folded it the same way. He pushed the fake one into the band of Wybourn's Stetson, trying to get it in the same place.

Footsteps sounded right outside the door. Tossing the Stetson back into place, Cullen lunged to his feet and was standing by his own bedroll when Hyde appeared in the doorway. The Southerner took no notice of Cullen but went straight to his own bedding and lay down.

Outside, Spragg and Hyde had been arguing.

'Iffen you knew yore hoss was in the corral, then you knew you was gonna scare it as much as the others,' Spragg told the other man. 'So iffen he don't come back, I reckons that be all yore fault,' he said with satisfied finality.

It was the last word too, for Hyde couldn't think of any adequate answer. Whiskers Spragg turned his back on the shootist to start putting up the corral poles again. Hyde stalked past the interested audience and went straight back to bed.

'Will we get the horses back?' Robinson asked Spragg.

'I 'spect so. Most likely the geldings'll be back afore long.' Spragg sighed. 'I shore hopes ol' Betty don't run off. She's a mighty fine team hoss, but she ain't got no more morals'n a two-bit whore.' Shaking his head over the mare's flighty tendencies, Spragg returned to the relative comfort of the only bunk.

★ ★ ★

As Spragg had predicted, four of the missing horses were waiting by the corral when the travellers rose the next morning. Hyde's liver chestnut was among them, nibbling thoughtfully on the withers of Solly, a bay gelding.

'No thanks to you,' muttered Hyde, going to catch his mount. 'Letting them all loose.'

'It was my hosses as brought yore fool critter back to this halt,' Whiskers Spragg returned, taking hold of a horse's forelock. 'You got sense enough to come right back here, ain't you, Solly?' he crooned to the horse. 'That fancy, go-to-town hoss ain't got no reason to come on back here.'

Hyde ignored the comment, which

was uncomfortably close to the truth. He slipped his bridle on to his horse and hitched it to the rails before checking it over.

Wilbur Jefferson approached Spragg. 'Ah can help yo' with the team hosses,' he offered. 'I'm mighty good with hosses, bless the Lawd. Mist' Boyd, he allus give me the bestest hosses in the stables to care for.' The black man grinned proudly, showing off his uneven teeth.

The wagon driver gave him a long look. 'I never let no slave handle my team afore.'

Jefferson shrugged. 'Why, Ah's a free man now. Ah doan' have to help yo' if you doan' want me to. An' yo' cain't make me work if I doan' want to.'

Spragg considered this. 'All right. We're like to be late startin' today.' He glanced at the sun as he spoke. 'I ain't never brought the coach in late yet. Let's be gettin' to work.'

'Sure thing.'

For all his impatience to start, Spragg

kept half an eye on the black man's work. Jefferson hadn't been boasting. He approached a chestnut mare with confidence, speaking to her in his mellow, low voice as he took her forelock and led her into the corral. Once there, he swiftly checked her over for cuts and strains, his wide, brown hands moving with calm sureness. The mare lowered her head and stood still for him. Spragg turned his full attention back to his own work.

At breakfast, Robinson was full of questions. He attacked the plateful of beans and eggs with vigour while he went over the events of the night.

'I swear, I was never so thrilled.' He tore off a lump of bread and mopped it among the beans and molasses. 'I really thought I was going to witness an attack by Indians.' The soggy bread was folded and stuffed into his mouth.

'I see that excitement doesn't spoil your appetite,' Cullen remarked. Robinson stared at him with naïve puzzlement.

'I'd like to have seen the wild horses,'

Mary Schmidt said wistfully. 'They must be so magnificent.'

'Not mustangs,' Cullen said. 'Most of them are plain scrub stock. Tough, but no picture.' He sipped the strong coffee.

'That's so,' Wybourn agreed graciously. 'I believe there may be good money to be made in breeding quality stock, if you pardon my mentioning the subject,' he added to Mary Schmidt.

She smiled, her gypsy eyes sparkling. 'I'm a farmer's wife, sir. I'm not going to faint at the mention of animal breeding.'

Cullen flashed her an admiring smile. 'You'd need a fair piece of range for raising horses though,' he went on. 'Still, if men like Wybourn get their way, and the Comanche are pushed back on to their little reservations, there'll be plenty of land available, and cheap at that. Maybe you should expand your business interests?' he suggested. His tone was easy but there was a cool curiosity in his eyes.

'My interests bring me a satisfactory income already,' Wybourn answered with dignity. He poured himself some more coffee. 'Perhaps you should take that opportunity yourself?'

Cullen shook his head. 'Me, breed range horses? No, I'm just an overweight travelling salesman, not some cowpoke.' He gestured at himself. 'I'm wearing a town suit, like you, not range duds.'

Further down the long table, Hyde's expression became thoughtful at that remark, but he said nothing. He just smiled to himself and sat quietly, eating the meal with little fuss.

★ ★ ★

By the time breakfast was over, even the flighty Betty had returned to the corral.

'Worthless li'l minx,' Spragg muttered, rubbing the mare around the ears. She lowered her head and fluttered her velvety nostrils at him. 'You' all's gonna make up for the time we lost today,' he warned his team as he started harnessing them. 'I ain't never been late an' I ain't plannin' to start now.'

With Jefferson's deft assistance, and some clumsier help from Robinson, the wagon was soon ready to leave Lone Cottonwood. Robinson was the last to climb aboard, clutching a basket of cold food which Betty-Lou MacKenzie had prepared for their lunch. He settled himself into his usual place as Spragg swung his whip high in the air.

'Get up there, you fool, owl-headed hosses,' he called. 'We got work to do.' The horses obeyed his commands and the wagon rolled back out on to the trail. Mary's chickens cackled as their coop began bouncing with the movement of the wagon.

Robinson squeezed between Cullen and Jefferson to get his elbows on the wagon box. 'What's today's run like?' he asked.

'Pretty damn dry,' the wagon driver

answered, pausing to spit tobacco juice at a scurrying hen. 'We're headin' on up through the Sierras. It's mighty grand scenery, iffen you like scenery.'

'If you don't like it, then why do you work out here?' Robinson asked shrewdly.

Spragg grunted, keeping his eyes on the team. 'Man kin work wherever he likes.'

'Of course,' Robinson answered diplomatically. 'Do you think we will encounter any Indians today?'

'I sure as hell hope not!'

'But is it likely?'

Mindful of the fact that Mary Schmidt could overhear them, Spragg said. 'It ain't so likely. Mebbe see a few traces of them, like yesterday.' The old frontiersman was more accurate than he knew.

'What about tonight's halt?' Robinson asked, rubbing a sore spot on his hip. 'Is there more than one bunk there?'

'Nope,' Whiskers Spragg answered with satisfaction. 'Ol' Baccy John ain't got more than a cot for hisself an' one for the wagon driver. You gotta sleep on the floor again.'

'I thought that might be the case.' Resignation tinged Robinson's tones as he withdrew inside the shade of the wagon again. Cullen grinned and patted his own generous stomach.

'You should put on a few pounds. There are times when my padding has its advantages.'

'Does it help with these benches?' Don Schmidt asked.

'Ain' nothin' could make these no more soft,' Jefferson drawled with feeling.

Although it was still early, the day was already hot. The passengers settled themselves as comfortably as they could, lulled into drowsiness by the heat and still air. Wybourn looked almost as immaculate as before, with just a thin trace of trail dust on his black suit, but he was the only one. Mary's bonnet was no longer crisp with starch; the thin strings were wilted and trailed down the front of her cheerful yellow dress. The men were soon sweating in the canvas-enclosed wagon. Robinson's hair had defeated the patent lotion and was curling defiantly. Cullen had abandoned his tie, derby hat and jacket and unfastened the soft shirt-collar. He didn't take off the underarm holster though.

After a while, Robinson could contain his curiosity no longer. He stirred on his hard bench, nudging his legs into Cullen's. The salesman woke from his dozy trance.

'Excuse me,' Robinson spoke quietly, leaning forward. 'May I examine your sidearm?'

'Sure, but make sure you point it at the floor of the wagon; it's full loaded.' Cullen handed over his revolver.

Robinson took it carefully, doing as he was told. He fitted his forefinger carefully through he trigger guard, gingerly squeezing the trigger until the slack had been taken up. He didn't notice that he was holding his breath. Cullen watched him carefully.

'Your hand's a mite big for that,' he said. 'An Army Colt like Hyde's would suit you better.'

'Mmmm. Is this a Colt?'

'No, just a copy of the Navy model, and I reckoned I was lucky to get issued that during the War.'

'You fought?' Robinson looked up with eager interest. He inadvertently lifted the gun too, pointing it straight at its owner for a moment, until he recalled himself and hastily pointed it again at the floorboards of the swaying wagon.

'Infantry,' Cullen said succinctly. 'Lots of mud but no glory.'

Robinson smothered a wistful sigh. The newspaper accounts and photographs of the War Between the States were what had inspired him to become a journalist. The War had ended before he could go report on it himself, and the veterans he had met since were often reluctant to talk about it. All of them seemed to stress the mud, hunger and disease. Robinson was gradually coming to the conclusion that war reporting might not have been as exciting as he had dreamed.

'How do I load it?' he asked, always eager for knowledge.

Cullen demonstrated, handling the gun with familiar ease.

'Should I purchase a revolver for my own protection while I'm travelling in the West?' Robinson asked.

Cullen nodded. 'You can use it to deal with predators, finish injured stock or signal for help.'

'What about fights and shoot-outs?' Robinson asked.

Cullen looked stern. 'Last resort only. Never draw a gun on another man unless you're prepared to kill him.'

Sitting beside the salesman, Jefferson was only half listening. His attention was on the view out the back of the wagon, and on Wybourn. The middle-aged man was listening intently, his head tilted to one side. His eyes were fixed on Cullen, and he was frowning.

After a few moments, he gave a tiny shake of his head and let his attention wander. Jefferson wondered about it, but didn't like to question the white man. It didn't seem important and he soon forgot what he'd seen.

The morning passed slowly. The passengers dozed or talked quietly. The hens had ceased fussing and even Robinson's energy seemed diminished. The wagon was crossing a wide stretch of dry mesa. Mountains in the distance were alluringly shaded with green, but there was little comfort on the trail. A fine cloud of white dust hung in the air, settling on clothes and sweaty skin. Cullen wiped his face frequently with his handkerchief.

Anxious though he was to make up for lost time, Spragg allowed the horses to slow to a walk. Their glossy coats were darkened in patches. Where the harness touched them, it whipped up the sweat to a white foam. Hyde slowed his horse too, riding a little way off to flank. His black jacket and

Stetson were greyed with dust and he had pulled his yellow neckerchief up over his nose and mouth.

After a couple of hours, Robinson could bear it no longer. Surging past Wybourn, he climbed over the tail-gate and dropped on to the faint tracks of the trail.

'What are you doing?' Don Schmidt called. The other passengers stirred and blinked at the noise.

'I came out here to see the frontier, and I'm not going to see much of it cooped up in there,' Robinson answered, walking along behind the stuffy wagon. His gait was a little stiff, but his long legs covered the ground quickly enough. 'At least railroads have glass windows, yeah, so you have a view as you travel.'

Up front, Spragg spat at a clump of ocotillo cactus whips. 'Iffen you admire the Goddamned railroads so much, whyn't you go haul yourself back East where they got them?'

'Because I want to see the frontier,

where they haven't got them,' Robinson yelled back.

Hyde grinned silently to himself. Spragg turned on the box to glare at Robinson, who had now moved up alongside the wagon.

'Iffen my wagon ain't good enough fer your fancy tastes, you can up an' walk to Black Horse halt.'

'I am walking,' Robinson pointed out stubbornly.

Cullen, leaning out on to the box, smiled admiringly. 'That fool overgrown greenhorn's sure got sand to burn,' he remarked to the wagon driver.

'I don't reckon to carry no man that insults my team,' Spragg grumbled.

'He wasn't insulting your team. He's fed up with how damn hot and airless it is in here, and he's got a point.' Cullen grabbed his derby, scrambled out on to the box and dropped down over the wheel. For a man of his bulk, he moved with quick grace. Letting the wagon pass, he crossed the trail and hurried to catch up with the tall newspaperman.

'Mighty fine weather we're having,' he remarked casually. Robinson goggled for a moment before bursting into laughter.

In spite of the baking sunshine overhead, it was good to feel the light wind that blew steadily across the mesa. Robinson squinted, trying to keep the dust out of his eyes. He'd about given up worrying about his clothes.

'Do you ever get used to this wind?' he asked plaintively.

'Nope, but you stop minding it after a while.' It was small comfort.

They trudged on steadily. Although Robinson didn't mind the exercise, he soon got thirsty and found himself thinking wistfully about lunch. A glance at his pocket watch showed him it was some time to noon yet. He tried to distract himself by examining the country they were passing through. Clumps of mesquite and creosote bush grew in the fine dirt, along with more types of cactus than he had ever imagined could exist. Scaled quail flew up almost from under his feet as he moved away from the faint wagon tracks. Robinson even glimpsed a jack rabbit scuttling away. Trying to trace its path, he got further away from the wagon.

'Hey!' Cullen's shout alerted him. 'Stick close to us.'

'Sure.' Robinson was smart enough to recognize the danger of getting cut off.

He was just turning back when he glimpsed water. A step forward revealed a decent-sized pool, with a few white clouds reflected in its still surface. Delighted, he bounded towards it.

'Robinson!' Cullen yelled again.

The gangly newspaperman turned and waved his hat in the air. 'I found some water!' he yelled back. 'I can get a good drink.'

'Shit,' Cullen muttered. Saving his breath, he broke into a run.

The people in the wagon heard the

shouting. 'What's happening?' Mary Schmidt asked.

'The Yankee gen'lman says he's found some water,' Jefferson told her, licking his lips at the thought of a cool drink.

Mary puzzled briefly over his thick drawl. 'Water? Oh, I'd just love to jump into a swimming hole right now.' She lurched forward as Spragg hauled his team to a sudden halt. 'What's wrong?' she cried.

Wybourn answered: 'About the only water out here is alkali water. If Robinson drinks it, it'll kill him.'

4

Cullen ran flat out over the seventy feet that separated him from Robinson, showing a surprising turn of speed for a man of his build. The young man had moved a few paces further away and crouched down. His dark curls were just visible above a prickly pear cactus. The pool of water was marvellously inviting in the June heat and dust. Robinson dipped his fingers in first, waving his hand about to let the water swirl round his fingers. It felt good against his dry skin. Kneeling, he leaned forward to dip both hands in.

'Stop! Don't!'

Robinson paused, water trickling through his cupped hands.

'No!' Cullen yelled as he raced closer.

Robinson glanced about, expecting to see painted savages rising from behind the cactus. The last of the water in his palms drained away and he shook his hands.

'What is it?' he called, wiping a deliciously cool hand over his dusty face.

'The water!' Cullen exclaimed. He slowed, gasping suddenly. The salesman jogged the last few yards and bent over, red in the face.

'Are you all right?' Robinson asked. 'What's wrong?' He cast anxious glances at the motionless wagon.

Thundering hooves drew his attention to Hyde, racing in from a patrol on the far side of the wagon. Hyde brought his horse to a halt, scattering stones and dust.

'What's the fuss?' he drawled, one hand resting on the butt of a gun.

Cullen lifted his head, still breathing heavily. 'Damn fool greenhorn there nearly drank alkali water.'

Robinson glanced back and forth, not understanding.

'I guess he didn't take any though,'

Hyde said calmly. He sat still on his horse, keeping a firm hold on the reins as it stretched its neck out to sniff at the water. He circled the liver chestnut away.

'I don't understand,' Robinson said. 'What's alkali water?'

'It's poisonous,' Hyde answered.

'It might look plumb good, but it's bitter,' Cullen added. 'You take a good drink of that, and you're like to be begging us to shoot you before you die.'

'But how can you tell it's alkali?' Robinson asked.

Cullen paused briefly before answering. 'Didn't you hear Spragg say this was a dry run? If there was good water hereabouts, he'd know about it.'

'I imagine so, yeah. Gee, thanks.' Robinson seized Cullen's hand and shook it vigorously.

'*De nada*,' Cullen answered casually, getting a curious look from Hyde. 'We'd best be getting back before that whiskery old-timer complains that we're making him late.'

'Sure.'

They were half-way back to the trail, when Robinson gave a whoop and scrambled under a creosote bush. He emerged a few moments later, twigs in his hair, proudly clutching an arrow.

'Look at this!' he held it up. 'I wonder how it got under there?'

'Not by accident.' Cullen took hold of Robinson's shirt sleeve and almost dragged him back to the wagon.

'Now what's holdin' you up?' yelled Spragg as they approached. 'You talks more'n a bunch of ladies at a quiltin' party.' He started to release the wagon's brake.

'Not yet,' Cullen said. He took the arrow from Robinson and handed it up to the driver's box.

Everyone clustered around; Hyde on his horse, the passengers leaning out of the wagon.

Spragg turned the arrow around until the single cock feather was pointing away from him. The dull steel arrowhead was horizontal.

'Comanche war arrow,' he said laconically. 'See, head's set on so's it'll go straight between your ribs. Barbed too, to make pullin' it out plumb miserable.'

'It doesn't appear to have been used,' Robinson said. 'Surely it's not just been discarded, yeah?'

Spragg squinted along the shaft to check its straightness. 'Nope; no Comanche'd waste a good arrow. See how straight the shaft is,' he said, holding it out for Robinson to examine. 'That's dogwood, with owl feathers. There ain't nothing to beat dogwood fer makin' arrows.'

Robinson traced the long grooves cut from feathers to point. The shaft was as smooth and perfect as if it had been machined in a factory back East.

'You'd never think that savages could make something so perfect,' he remarked.

'Let me see,' Mary Schmidt pleaded.

The young man reluctantly handed it over to her.

Spragg snorted. 'Savages! Well, mebbe they be so, but that don't mean they be stupid. And them savages be plannin' something mighty big afore long.'

'And we're likely to be right in the middle of it,' Cullen added. His round, pleasant face was uncommonly serious.

Spragg started to explain. 'An arrow under a bush like that is tellin' other scouts about a war council bein' held someplace. About how far from the centre of the bush were it?'

'About seven inches.'

'They're meetin' mebbe seven miles from here.'

Hyde swung down from his horse and touched Cullen on the shoulder. They withdrew a few paces to speak quietly.

'Do you reckon Spragg knows what he's talking about?' Hyde asked. 'Why, I don't doubt he knows Indians, but I've heard tell that different tribes do things differently. He's talking about Comanches, but aren't those Pawnee moccasins he's wearing?'

Cullen shook his head. 'They're Comanche all right, and good ones too. Look at those long heel-fringes, and the tin decorations.'

'Oh.' Hyde's grey eyes gleamed as he looked at Cullen. Just how did that plump salesman come to know so much about frontier life and Indians? Was he really a salesman? As Cullen was turning to join the others, Hyde coughed discreetly.

'By the way,' he said. 'I'd sure admire to see some of the samples of yours. I know a fine lady back in New Orleans who'd look real swell in them.'

Cullen grinned suddenly. 'Sure. But these aren't such fine goods; cotton and muslin, not silk.'

Hyde revealed his sharklike smile. 'Well, she isn't such a very fine lady. Real taking though.'

'I'll bet. Maybe you should give me her address. I always wanted a good reason to visit New Orleans.'

'Later.'

Cullen winked, then wiped the smile off his face as he rejoined the group at the front of the wagon.

After a little more discussion, Whiskers Spragg ordered them back inside so he could press on.

'Giddap there, hosses,' he bellowed. 'Let's be movin' on afore them Comanche come take a fancy to our scalps.'

* * *

By noon, the wagon had descended into a wide, shallow canyon. Rustling trees gave shade, and a clear creek ran across the floor. When Spragg announced that they were back on schedule, even Robinson didn't bother checking his watch to confirm the time. They settled down for a welcome rest. Mary produced a checked tablecloth from her trunk and spread the cold food on it. There was fried chicken, sourdough

93

biscuits, bread, cold potatoes and some currant bread.

'That cloth gives real tone to our picnic,' Cullen told Mary, his blue eyes flirting with her. 'I wish I got to travel with ladies more often.'

'I bets I makes better coffee'n her,' Spragg insisted. 'Womenfolks allus makes it too weak.'

'That's as maybe, but you couldn't bring tone to a pack of mangy coyotes,' Cullen told him.

Mary laughed with delight, her rosebud mouth flowering with mirth. Don Schmidt stared at Cullen with a mixture of jealousy and admiration. Shyly, he took his young wife's hand as they sat together.

Robinson was opposite them, his long legs crossed untidily. He ate left-handedly, meanwhile writing in the notebook balanced on one knee. The arrow lay in front of him, a precious souvenir to be added to the misshapen bullet, and the buffalo-scrotum tobacco-pouch bought in Independence. As the meal progressed, he drew out Spragg on the topic of Indian life and the endless uses the Comanches had for buffaloes.

'We saw great herds of buffalo on our way south,' Mary Schmidt put in. Her husband nodded agreement.

Spragg looked wise. 'Sure you did; but hunters is startin' to move in on 'em. All they want's the hide, an' the rest rots.'

'The fewer buffalo there are, the fewer Indians there will be in the future,' Wybourn stated.

Mary frowned. 'It doesn't seem right somehow.'

'If they can't hunt, they will have to learn to farm like civilized people,' Wybourn told her. 'It will be for their own good in the end. This is a tough world, and I believe that only those willing to fight and work will make their way in it.'

'Some people believe that we don't have the right to tell the Indians how to live, yeah?' Robinson said.

As the argument developed, Cullen got up quietly and slipped away. He walked over to the wagon and climbed inside. Only Hyde noticed him go. The wagon was stuffy inside, as the canvas curtains were still down. Cullen moved carefully, light on his feet in the cluttered space. He crouched between two of the bench-seats and reached under the rear one. Wybourn's bag was stored there, as it had been since leaving Fort Stockton. The back of the wagon was angled away from the fire, so Cullen couldn't see the others. Drawing Wybourn's bag out, he examined the brass lock on the strap. He got out his penknife and selected the narrowest blade. A few moments of careful jiggling paid off. After another quick look out, Cullen opened up Wybourn's bag. It was an expanding one, like a carpet-bag, but made of good leather. Cullen handled it carefully, disturbing the contents as little as possible as he searched. His mild face wore a serious look as he felt the neatly folded clothes. Some paper crackled, and he drew it out swiftly. He unfolded it and read, his eyes darting quickly over the words. It wasn't what he was looking for. There was real bitterness in his face as he lowered the sheet.

'Does Wybourn keep fal-de-dals in his bag too?'

Cullen started at Hyde's drawl. The quiet man had climbed up the front of the wagon and was leaning in from the driver's box. As Cullen glared at him, Hyde climbed right in.

'I don't recall that one being yours,' he remarked with mild curiosity.

'I've got a good reason,' Cullen said.

'I'm sure.' Hyde sat down. He watched the salesman steadily, but didn't bother keeping his hands by his guns.

'It involves justice,' Cullen said. 'And money.'

'They can drive a man to many things.'

'If I get what I want, there'll be money enough to share,' Cullen said frankly.

Hyde smiled to himself. 'You done met Wybourn before?'

Cullen shook his head. Hyde sat absolutely still, but the salesman was on edge, still holding the sheet of paper clutched in his hand. He seemed to realize suddenly that he was crushing it, for he laid the paper on the bench in front of him and smoothed it down compulsively.

'Well, you're not just a fancy salesman,' Hyde remarked, his grey eyes studying the other man. 'Why, you've lived on the frontier plenty. I just bet you've been out here before now.'

'I grew up out in Texas,' Cullen admitted. Life suddenly flashed back into his face. 'My pappy travelled around a lot always looking for some-place new; new ways of making some *dinero*. I never saw the inside of a school till I was turned twelve. Hell, I didn't see *any* school until I was twelve. I'd lived in fifteen different places by then.'

'Our family lived on our plantation for nigh on seventy years,' Hyde said, more to himself than the other man. His face hardened at memories, and he fell silent again.

'We both lost in the War,' Cullen said. 'I've been chasing my inheritance four years, and I've never been so goddamn close.' His hands closed to fists as he spoke. 'I will get justice.'

Hyde lifted his head suddenly, like an alert hound. 'Someone's coming,' he warned.

Cullen acted first and spoke second. Sliding the paper back into its proper place, he said: 'I'll give you the medicine on this tonight. Like I said, there's money in this.'

'Right.'

Cullen snapped the lock closed on the bag, making Hyde suddenly wonder how he had got it open, and shoved the bag back under its bench. By the time Jefferson peered over the tail-gate, Hyde had climbed out again and Cullen was sorting through his bag of samples. He looked up innocently, a frilly thing dangling from one hand.

'You ever seen a lady wearing one of these?' he asked, his eyes sparkling.

'Nope. An' Ah reckons that iffen she wears sech a thing as that, she one mighty wicked lady.' Jefferson paused for effect. 'An' I sure wish the Lawd would gimme a lady like that.'

'Amen.'

★ ★ ★

The afternoon journey was quietly tense. Spragg pushed the horses on, wanting to reach the safety of Black Horse halt. At least among the slopes of the Sierras there was a fresher breeze and patches of shade. At Mary Schmidt's request, the canvas sides of the wagon were rolled up. The views were spectacular. The trail climbed steadily, sometimes dipping into canyons and draws. Steep walls of rock rose around them, crowned with stands of cool green pine. The lower slopes were open, dotted with creosote bush, rabbit bush and dozens of cacti. Robinson asked endless questions about the plants and animals they saw.

'Look up there.'

A call from Hyde alerted them to bighorn sheep standing on a ledge above them. Mary Schmidt leaned sideways to see them, pressing herself close to Robinson.

'They're magnificent!' she exclaimed as the sheep bounded away along the tiny ledge on the canyon wall.

'A set of them horns would sure make a dandy souvenir,' Wybourn remarked to Robinson.

'Oh, yes. Could we stop to shoot one?' he asked, peering around the flared brim of Mary's bonnet.

She realized she was almost in his arms and sat upright again hurriedly. Cullen caught her eye and winked.

She stared right back, refusing to be flustered.

'We ain't got time,' Spragg answered. 'Besides, them sheep is more cussed than any woman.' He spat over the side of the wagon. 'They ain't never where you wants them to be.'

Robinson accepted the refusal good-naturedly. Looking across to the other side of the broad canyon, he saw something flashing. A moment later it was there again.

'What's that?' He pointed. 'I believe I saw a light flashing from up there.'

It came again, two rapid blinks of brilliant light from high on the rim.

'Comanches are watching us,' Cullen said quietly.

'Is that their signals? How are they doing it?'

'Reflecting sunlight off a bit of glass or mirror.'

Robinson's eyes widened. 'A helio-graph? But that's very sophisticated; yeah?' He stopped and laughed at himself. 'I know, savage doesn't necessarily mean stupid.'

'That's sure right, boy,' Scragg answered.

'But do that mean they's goin' ter jump us?' Jefferson asked, screwing himself round on the wooden bench to look at Spragg.

'Nope. Not jest yet.'

'If they were, they wouldn't chance letting us see the signal,' Cullen explained.

'Thas mighty comfortin'.' Jefferson spoke so dead-pan that no one knew whether he was joking.

Spragg shook the reins and urged his team on a little better.

* * *

Everyone was looking forward to their arrival at Black Horse halt. The Easterners longed for the security of stout adobe walls between themselves and wild Indians. Spragg was keen to pick up a fresh team of horses for the last leg of the journey. Everyone was looking forward to a rest from the hard benches, and some hot food.

Spragg was the first to know that there was something wrong. He saw the half-dozen buzzards wheeling in the blue sky. The halt itself wasn't in sight yet. The trail had to wind around the bulge of a dry hill before the land opened out. Two of the buzzards dropped out of view and didn't come back. There was nothing to scare them from landing by the halt. Spragg caught Hyde's eye and gestured at the birds. The quiet man nodded, and loosened his Winchester in its boot. Spragg lifted his shotgun across his lap, steadying it with his right hand while his left controlled the six horses. Wybourn opened the jacket he still wore in spite of the heat, tucking it behind his holster. Cullen had removed his jacket hours ago. He became quieter and more alert.

The weary team rounded the last corner at a steady pace. Heavy black birds flapped up into the sky and a coyote dashed into cover.

'Goddamn it,' Spragg said softly. 'Goddamn them all.' The adobe was burnt out, the solid, blackened walls still standing. The corral was untouched but empty, the gate hanging wide open. Something lay on the dirt near the gate.

Spragg reined the team to a halt without getting any closer. Hyde stopped some ten yards distant. Mary Schmidt leaned forward.

'What is it?' she asked.

Cullen hastily blocked her view. 'Don't look out there. The Comanches have already been.'

'Oh.' She sat back suddenly, raising her hand to her mouth.

'Is they still here?' Jefferson whispered. He was holding the long axe that had been stowed under his seat.

'We're gonna scout round some afore gettin' closer,' Spragg said, climbing nimbly down from the box. He directed the men swiftly, sending Hyde and Cullen around one way, while he went the other with Wybourn.

'What about me?' Robinson asked, slightly nettled. 'I used to take my paw's shotgun out hunting.'

'Stay by the wagon and keep yer eyes open,' Spragg told him. 'You ain't rangewise, an' that's what we be needin' now.'

'Here.' Hyde offered the young man one of his Colts.

'Thanks.'

As the other men moved away. Robinson organized the group by the wagon. He had the canvas sides rolled down and ordered Mary Schmidt to lie on the floor. Jefferson and Don Schmidt he stationed on either side as look-outs, while he stood next to the box.

The precautions were unnecessary. No one had any doubt that Comanches were still in the area, but there was no immediate danger of ambush.

'Stay or push on?' Cullen asked, looking at the other men gathered around the wagon. 'Comanches don't like fighting in the dark.'

'We could cover quite a distance before sun-up, yeah?' Robinson said.

'Nothin' a Comanch' scout on a good relay couldn't do afore breakfast,' Spragg said. ' 'Sides which, my team need them a rest an' a good feed.' He stroked the quarters of the nearest horse.

His point was a good one. This morning the team had been eager and glossy-coated. Now they stood quietly in the harness, heads low, their hides dull with sweat and dirt.

'We'll take watches then,' Wybourn proposed. 'With seven of us to spell each other, we should all get some good rest.' The other men were nodding agreement until Robinson spoke up. 'I don't think Spragg should stay awake,' he said. As the old man started to sputter, Robinson rushed out the rest of his thoughts. 'He's the driver, and I doubt whether anyone else could handle the team as well as he does, yeah? We may need all his skills tomorrow. He should get some proper rest.'

'Young fool greenhorn!' Whiskers Spragg drew himself up to his full height, which brought him about level with Robinson's chin. 'I ain't needing so much sleep as you young fellers! I kin take my turn.'

'Why, Robinson's right, and you know it,' Hyde told him, his grey eyes sparkling with amusement at the whiskered driver's indignation. 'I'll take first watch with Cullen, then Robinson and Jefferson. Wybourn and Don can take the last shift together.'

Spragg snorted, but stopped arguing. 'We'll plant ol' Baccy John an' fix the place up some,' he said. 'You got such a thing as a shovel in that mess of tools?' he asked Don Schmidt.

'Sure we have,' answered Mary, who had been leaning over the side to listen. She fetched it from its place under the bench seats and started to climb out with it.

Whiskers Spragg took it from her. 'You'd better stay clear a whiles, ma'am. It sure ain't no sight for a woman.' Mary didn't answer, but climbed back into the wagon to wait.

Manual labour was beneath Spragg's dignity as a coach driver, but he wouldn't permit anyone else to dig the grave for his old friend's body. As he worked, the other men saw to the horses, and used more of the Schmidts' tools to repair the burnt-out house. Robinson put his height to good use, fixing a tarpaulin over the charred beams to make a roof. Baccy John's rifle, blankets and shot had gone, but Don found a sack of beans, some dried fish and two tins of peaches. Cullen helped where needed, but he was quieter than usual. He took a look at Baccy John's body before the burial, and was relieved to see that the old man hadn't been killed by a repeating rifle.

It was still a simple fact that Black Dog's warriors had the confidence to roam around the country, killing and stealing as they wished. Cullen thought of the rifle receipt tucked in his clothes, and of Wybourn's wish for the Army to clear the marauding Comanches from the land. They stood on opposite sides of the shallow grave as Robinson read a prayer. Wybourn was holding his Stetson in his hands, his head bowed reverently as he listened. Cullen didn't close his eyes for the prayers, but watched Wybourn steadily. The older man never blushed or showed unease.

Afterwards, they all returned to the battered adobe. The iron stove had survived the fire relatively undamaged, so Mary fixed them a hot meal, washed down with Spragg's strong coffee.

There was little talk among the travellers as they settled themselves for the night. The adobe hut had two rooms. Mary and Don had taken the little room at the back; the rest of the party had picked spots on the floor of the larger one. Spragg's dented coffeepot stayed warm on the sooty stove as the resting men slid into sleep.

Cullen and Hyde stayed on opposite

sides of the room, peering now and then through the empty window spaces. The charred remains of the door had been cleaned away and broken up for firewood. A group of coyotes sang dissonantly somewhere in the distance. Even after three years out west, the eerie noise still sent shivers up Hyde's spine. There were other sounds closer to hand; gentle snores, the regular noises of frogs in the sluggish creek, muffled sounds of horses in the corral. Over an hour passed as Hyde listened to the night sounds, before he crossed silently to Cullen.

The salesman turned to him, meeting his gaze evenly. There was just enough light in the room for them to see objects on the floor, but it was dim enough to make reading expressions hard.

'Explain,' Hyde said softly.

Cullen nodded, trying to choose where to start. 'I said I never met Wybourn afore, and that's true enough. But he rode in the War alongside my pappy. Pappy and I used to write each other, best we could, and he told me about Wybourn.' He sat down and levered off his right boot. Hyde flicked glances at him as he listened, most of his attention on keeping watch.

Slipping his fingers inside the long boot, Cullen produced two folded papers from a hidden compartment. He stood up and handed one to Hyde, then pushed his foot back into the boot.

'That's one of Pappy's letters about Wybourn,' he said.

Hyde carefully unfolded the worn paper and peered at it in the dim light, while Cullen kept watch. As the salesman had promised, his father mentioned Jack Wybourn, and his skill with the Navy Colt he wore.

'Do you favour your pa?' Hyde asked, folding the letter and giving it back. 'I've seen Wybourn look at you like he done met you someplace before.'

'I'm some like him,' Cullen admitted. 'And Momma says I sure sound like he done.' A smile showed briefly on his rounded face before he went on. 'Pappy's name was Williams but I don't want Wybourn to catch on. Cullen's my middle name, it's my momma's maiden name. Like I said, Pappy was one for seeing new places. Just before the War started, I was clerking in San Antonio, keeping the family, whiles Pappy went prospecting in the Sierra Blancas.'

'Prospecting?' Hyde repeated the key word, but there was no excitement in his voice.

'Sure. And he found silver.' Bitterness leaked into Cullen's tone. 'Then we went to War with the Yankees right after he wrote us about it. Pappy enlisted right away without even coming home. And after that, he never dared send us his map, in case it got stole or lost in the War.'

'You couldn't get into the same unit?' Hyde asked.

'Nope. I didn't join up till sixty-three, when Louisa turned fifteen and got teaching work to keep the family. Pappy was killed in some little skirmish

113

in Arkansas, four months after. His captain done sent us his watch and a tintype of the family he had, but we never got the map. The captain also wrote us that Jack Wybourn was with Pappy when he took lead, and carried him away over his saddle.'

Cullen steadily unfolded the second paper and held it out. 'I wrote Wybourn after the War, asking if he'd seen Pappy's map. He said not.'

Like the first letter, this one had been kept carefully folded through the years. Hyde took it gently, reading the few lines of neat copperplate. He wasn't surprised to find that it was exactly as Cullen claimed.

'Wybourn could be telling the truth,' he remarked, handing the letter back.

Cullen smiled bleakly. 'He could. But he never came to El Paso afore the War. He's visited plenty the last two years. Bought himself into the bank; got a little boarding-house run by an old woman that talks too much. She don't take none to the half-breed that visits

Wybourn there sometimes. Wybourn claims they go hunting together, but he never fetches much meat back.' He paused, and looked straight at the other man. 'I aim to search Wybourn's things for that map tonight. Are you going to stop me?'

5

Hyde shook his head. 'My mammy always told me never get between a man and his obsession.'

Cullen's face warmed into a faint smile before he turned to pick his way between the sleeping men.

Wybourn had taken the place closest to the stove, though it was a warm enough night. His greying hair showed against his black hat, which he was using as a pillow. Cullen took the pocket-book from Wybourn's jacket and retreated with it back to the doorway. There, in the faint starlight, he searched the contents thoroughly. Apart from cash, all he found was a letter to the El Paso bank, asking for $500 to buy land. After showing it to Hyde, he carefully returned the pocket-book.

His face was tight with frustration.

Still determinedly searching, Cullen carefully felt the rest of Wybourn's suit jacket. A piece of paper proved to be no more than a scrap with a lawyer's name on it. There was a box of sulphur matches, two keys and a pocket-comb; nothing more. Cullen felt his way around the lapels in case anything should have been sewn inside but there was nothing.

He was running out of places to search and there was still no map. Cullen rocked back on to his heels and thought for a moment. The jacket hung in his hands, weighted down by odds and ends like the fancy cigar case. Cullen's face lit up with sudden hope. His careful fingers extracted the cigar case from the pocket. Inside was nothing but half a dozen fine cigars. For a moment Cullen wanted to hurl the silver case clear across the room. He lifted it sharply but halted himself. Even in the dim light, his silent anger was clear enough to Hyde. Cullen swallowed the fury, grateful for the darkness that hid his face. He closed the cigar-case and put it back, silently trying to compose himself.

'Nothing,' he reported back to Hyde as he joined him by the door. 'I can't find a single damn thing to show you.'

His very behaviour had convinced the Southerner of his seriousness. Something was up, and Hyde saw the chance to make himself some money.

'I reckon there'll be other chances later,' he drawled.

Cullen nodded absently. He was wondering whether to show Hyde the receipt he'd found. 'Wybourn sure seems keen to see the Comanche driven on to the reservation,' he remarked.

'Why, it'd make life a whole lot safer out here,' Hyde said. 'It could be dangerous out at the mine, if it's in Indian country,' he added disingenuously, showing his shark-like smile. 'You'd need someone who's handy with firearms to protect you.'

'I guess,' Cullen answered. His plans

hadn't got as far as practical details of running a mine. His attention was devoted solely to getting his father's map back. He made up his mind to keep the secret about the receipt a while longer.

'Maybe he keeps the map locked in a safe in town,' Hyde suggested. 'It's a mighty valuable thing to be carrying round.'

'Perhaps. But I'm plumb sure he's got it hid someplace. I aim to get me that map or die trying. I've got some savings behind me; I'll pay you five hundred dollars to back me up.'

That was far more than Hyde had hoped for, but nothing showed on his face. He just nodded.

'You'd best get over to the window. We got a reason to be on watch here, remember?' he drawled.

'Sure.'

The rest of their watch passed quietly. After another couple of hours, they shook Robinson and Jefferson awake, and settled down in their bedrolls.

Robinson didn't enjoy being woken from his rest, but the excitement of keeping watch against dangerous Indians made up for it. Sometimes he patrolled from window to door, peering into the dim light and listening to the fascinating night sounds of the open range. Most of the time he stood with his elbows on the window-sill and mentally tried out material for the next letter to his editor. Jefferson kept watch patiently from his own side of the room.

He was the first to notice a dark shape moving out near the wagon. Jefferson leaned forward to get a better view. The night was full of shadows that changed with the thin clouds as they passed the moon. The bulk of the wagon and outline of the corral were both clear enough from where he was. A darker shadow had appeared near the rear wheel of the wagon. Jefferson watched longer, unwilling to raise a false alarm. Sure enough, the shadow moved. It slipped forward, soundless, and paused again by the front wheels of the wagon. There it stretched upward, taking the unmistakable shape of a man peering over the wagon box.

Jefferson stepped quietly back from the window, then hurried across the room. 'Mist' Robinson!' he hissed.

Robinson started, and came back to his immediate surroundings.

'What?'

'Ah kin see Injuns, suh. Ah reckons they's goin' to steal the hosses.'

'Then we'd better stop them, yeah?'

Robinson covered the distance to the door in a couple of long strides. He peered out, saw a dim figure crossing the open space to the corral, and raised the gun he'd been lent. He held the Colt shoulder high and fired without stopping to think. Flame lashed from the barrel as the gun kicked against his palm. Over the noise, Robinson was surprised to hear a scream of pain.

'I hit him!' he exclaimed, dazzled by the gun flare. Still blinking, he

121

ran forward, eager to find out what he'd done.

Back in the adobe, others were waking up fast. Hyde rolled free from his quilts, his Winchester in his hands even before he was upright. Cullen, Spragg and Wybourn woke and started to rise, all with hands on weapons. There were no calls or sounds of confusion in the dark room.

Robinson was completely taken aback when guns started firing somewhere out in the darkness. He stopped dead, remembering to raise the Colt and thumb back the hammer. He could just about make out the man he had hit, who was trying to crawl back to the wagon. He glimpsed flashes in the darkness as rifles were fired at him. Only when a bullet cracked right past his ear, did Robinson abruptly understand how reckless he had been.

'Jesus!' Firing off the gun, he flung himself full length on to the ground.

Hyde reached the window and peered out cautiously.

'What's happening?' Spragg demanded. The old-timer had his shotgun ready.

'That fool greenhorn's gone and shot himself an Indian,' Hyde drawled. 'Now they got him pinned down out there.' Even as he spoke, he was aiming the Winchester.

The wounded Comanche was trying to escape. Another figure slipped from the shadows to help. Comanches would never leave their dead or injured behind if they could help it. A volley of fire opened up from the adobe. The brave ducked and weaved as he ran to help his friend. Bullets sang around him but he put faith in his medicine and his courage.

Still lying in the open, Robinson raised his head enough to see what was happening. He was so engrossed in watching the drama barely thirty feet away that he forgot all about the gun he had dropped in his panic. The Comanches were almost naked, wearing nothing more than moccasins and breechclouts. Their coppery skins made them hard to see in the darkness. The injured one struggled to his feet, one hand clutched against his side. Even though he staggered, he made no sound or groan. Robinson was briefly disappointed that neither one wore crowns of feathers like the Indians in George Catlin's pictures. But these were clearly young men, lithe and powerful.

A bullet kicked up dirt barely a foot from Robinson's head, but he never noticed. The rescuer reached his friend unhurt. Without wasting a word, he bent and lifted the other Comanche over his own shoulders. He had barely taken two paces before a bullet hit him. He staggered, but held on to his burden. Robinson held his breath as he watched, willing the daring rescuer on.

Inside the adobe, Hyde worked the lever action of his Winchster in a blur of speed. He fired steadily at the indistinct, moving target.

'Goddamn it!' Spragg swore, leaning

so close to Hyde that the smell of black tobacco was noticeable even through the gunpowder. 'They's aimin' fer my hosses.'

Two more Comanches had appeared in the night, running for the gate of the corral. It was set to one side of the house, and was only partially visible from the window. Spragg ran to the back of the house, brushing recklessly through the blanket that hung in the door between the two rooms. There was a squeal of surprise from Mary Schmidt as the old-timer burst into her bedroom.

'Beg pardon,' Spragg muttered absently, making for the window.

Mary sat upright among the blankets on the floor, her long braid of hair trailing over her white nightgown. Don was beside her, clutching her arm in the confusion.

Spragg leaned through the window holes, braced the shotgun against his shoulder and fired off a blast. One of the Comanches stumbled and fell.

'Get out of it, you son of a bitch!' Spragg bellowed, thumbing back the other hammer. 'You ain't gettin' none of my team, you stinkin' hoss raiders.' He let the other barrel loose.

'Sir!' Don protested futilely. 'Mind your language in front of my wife!'

'Oh, hush up,' Mary snapped, untangling herself from the blankets and her husband.

'Where are you going?' he exclaimed, grabbing for the hem of her nightgown and missing.

'Someone might get hurt. I can't shoot but I can bandage.' With that parting remark, Mary hurried into the confusion of the main room.

Spragg grinned at the disconcerted husband as he reloaded the shotgun. 'That wife o' your'n sure got some gumption.'

Don Schmidt merely gaped back, wondering what had happened to the quiet woman he had wooed back in Ohio.

Robinson suddenly realized that he

was in real trouble. Dirt sprayed into his face as a bullet struck just in front of him. He could see the two nearest Comanches, both wounded now, and another by the corral. As his mind became alive to the situation, he realized there were at least two more in the clump of trees near the creek; both were firing at him. He gathered himself to rise, only to hear the crack of guns from behind. If he stood up, he risked getting shot by his friends back in the adobe.

Completely alert to danger, he saw one of the injured Comanches crawling towards him. Moonlight gleamed off the blade of a knife held ready to attack. Injured as he was, the brave intended to take a coup and die with glory.

'Wait! Stop!' Robinson remembered the gun and cast about frantically for it.

Seeing his panic, the Comanche gathered his strength to rush forward. He raised his knife and howled out his war-cry. The fearsome wail terrified Robinson. The young man froze like a startled jack rabbit.

Hyde had noticed the injured buck creeping closer but hadn't been able to get a clear shot at him. Wybourn was at the other window and Cullen was taking careful shots around the door frame, but their pistols didn't have enough range to make certain hits. When Robinson cried out in panic, Hyde acted. He left the window and raced for the door, stepping through as he raised the Winchester to shoulder-height. Cullen fired off his last two shots as cover. The Comanche shrieked his war-cry just as Hyde shot. Robinson saw the brave jerk, then drop without another sound. He simply crumpled, like a horse shot in the head. The sight jerked Robinson from his frozen panic. He dropped to the ground again and started shuffling backwards.

Hyde knew his shot had hit. He worked the lever action again and again, mechanically counting his shots as he covered Robinson's retreat. He took a step backards, still firing into the dark with his eyes half closed against the glare from his own gun. Then something heavy tore at his arm. Hyde cried out without knowing it, almost dropping his rifle. Someone grabbed his collar and he was hauled back into safety. His head was still spinning as he found himself leaning against the inner wall of the adobe.

'What?' The question was slurred.

Mary Schmidt had appeared from somewhere and was cutting away the sleeve of his cotton shirt. Warm blood poured down his arm and the pain hit suddenly. Hyde gritted his teeth and rested his head back against the wall.

'They're quitting,' said someone. The voice sounded a long way away.

'An' they didn't get themselves nothin' but lead and powder.' That sounded like Spragg. Hyde decided that the others had everything under control. He sat silently and let Mary bandage his torn arm. Her hands were gentle and soothing as she worked.

'Can you move your fingers?' she asked eventually.

Hyde opened his eyes and looked at her. The concern on her sweet face was as refreshing as a cup of coffee.

'I reckon so,' he answered, trying his hand. 'Why, that ain't so bad.' The bullet had torn through his upper arm, his left arm luckily, but hadn't hit the bone. It would heal up readily enough.

'I'm glad.' Mary patted him on the knee and got up to see what else was happening. Hyde smirked, and stayed where he was, listening to the babble of conversation.

'They were using repeaters,' Cullen was saying. 'Not one or two, but four at least.'

'It sounded that way,' Wybourn answered. His face was faintly flushed, but there was a tightness around his eyes that suggested anger, not shame.

'I shot one of them,' Robinson said proudly. He lifted his hand and mimed his actions. 'I hit him first time and he rolled right over.'

'Chance,' snorted Wybourn.

'It was not!' Robinson exclaimed. He pulled himself up to his full, impressive height, puffing his chest out. 'A chancy shot would never hit in conditions like those. It was natural skill with firearms.'

Cullen grinned at the left-handed logic.

'Why, you've got no more skill with firearms than I do with a steam engine,' Hyde interrupted scornfully.

'I disagree with you.' Robinson ran his hand through his hair, disordering the unruly curls.

'You going to show me it wasn't chance?' Hyde drawled.

'Certainly. Here and now if you wish.' Robinson stood firm on his dignity.

'You don't have to make a plumb fool of yourself,' Cullen told him. 'We all enjoy it, but it isn't necessary.'

'I shall stand by my boast like a

man,' Robinson answered. 'Or at least, I shall try my best,' he added more honestly.

'This I just gotta see!' Cullen exclaimed. He extended an arm to help Hyde to his feet. 'The gauntlet has been thrown down and the challenge accepted. Say, Jefferson, fetch those tin cans that had peaches in them, would you?'

With Cullen's renewed energy behind it, the challenge was swiftly organized. Robinson found himself standing thirty feet away from a row of empty tins and bottles. He could see them in the moonlight, but judging the exact distance was tricky. Everyone was there watching him, except Spragg, who was in the corral grumbling to his restless horses.

'Ladies and gentlemen,' Cullen announced in the florid style of a fairground barker. 'Roll up, roll up. Come and see Hulton F. Robinson, sterling young newspaperman of Rhode Island, perform his miraculous trick shooting. For your entertainment, he will attempt, in the dark, to shoot not four, not five, but six targets.' He finished with a theatrical flourish and a bow. Mary applauded.

Robinson cast a martyred look at the salesman, then lifted the gun he had borrowed. Holding his breath, he aimed and fired. There was a distinct clang as the endmost tin spun and fell. It was followed by genuine gasps of amazement from the audience. Robinson was just as surprised, but kept up his fierce concentration. His second shot missed. The third shattered a bottle into fragments. Robinson lowered the Colt a moment and made himself breathe slowly. At least he wasn't going to make a complete and utter fool of himself. The fourth shot thudded into the chopping block. The fifth struck a tin, sending it bouncing across the ground. His last shot missed, but Robinson was too pleased with himself to care.

'I told you I could shoot, yeah?' he

said triumphantly. 'I managed three out of six, yeah?'

'Why it was nothing more than beginner's luck!' Hyde exclaimed. 'And you took so long about it.'

'I never claimed to be any shootist,' Robinson answered rather smugly. He held the gun out to the outraged man. 'Thank you for the loan of your firearm.'

By this time, the rest of the audience were on the point of open laughter. Mary Schmidt, with a cloak thrown over her nightgown, was clinging to her husband's hand as she stifled squeaks of mirth. Jefferson was chuckling, and Cullen was trying to muffle involuntary snorts of laughter. Even Wybourn couldn't help smiling. Hyde snatched his Colt back off the newspaperman.

'Set up them bottles again and I'll show you-all what a real shootist can do.'

His defiant stance lost a little dignity when he was forced to ask Cullen to reload his gun for him. The salesman obliged, careful to keep the smile off his face, although he couldn't suppress the sparkle in his eyes. Nor could he resist the chance to make a production of Hyde's shots.

'Ladies and gentlemen. This is a unique opportunity for you to see Mr Hyde, formerly of the Confederate States Cavalry, taking part in a public display of gunmanship.' Cullen gestured towards the glowering figure, standing stiff and still beside him. 'Mr Hyde here will attempt to better the record set by the challenger, Hulton F. Robinson, of Rhode Island. And remember, Hyde is handicapped by a recent injury, but will make the attempt anyhow. Your applause for his courage.' He wound up with another bow. This time, Mary, Don and Jefferson all applauded.

'He's brave to make the attempt,' Don whispered to Mary.

'Bull-headed as a pair of mules, the both of them,' she answered quietly.

Hyde couldn't imagine how he had got into this situation, but he was bound and determined to get this nonsense over with. He took a good look at the targets; only five this time since one of the bottles had been shattered. When he was confident in his own mind, he acted. By his own standards, he shot slowly, but he was much faster than Robinson. Five shots rang out in ten seconds. Three tins and one bottle leapt into the air. The other bottle stayed on the chopping block. Hyde lowered the Colt, steadfastly ignoring dizziness and the pain in his left arm.

'Four,' he said quietly, turning.

'That's only one more than I got, yeah?' Robinson said with unabashed delight.

'Why, there was one less target for me,' Hyde argued. He slid the gun back into its holster, and supported his injured arm.

'But I've hardly held a gun before, and I scored almost as much as you.' Robinson beamed down at Hyde, who was above average height himself and not used to being looked down at.

Hyde's temper flared up. 'I shot much faster than you did,' he insisted.

'You didn't say it was a speed match.'

The argument was abruptly interrupted. 'What in th' name of God is goin' on here?' Whiskers Spragg stumped over to the two men. 'Why're you two whittle-whanging away out here in the dark? Why, there's prob'ly Comanches out there right now, like to bust a gut with laughin' at yer.'

Hyde turned on him. 'The tenderfoot there said he could shoot as well as I can.' He jabbed a finger towards the chopping block. Spragg turned to look. He gave a snort of derision, then with one swift movement, he unslung the shotgun from his shoulder, and blew away the remaining bottle. It exploded into fragments which scattered far and wide round the chopping block.

'That's shootin',' Spragg said. 'Now quit scarin' the hosses and git back ter bed.' Slinging the shotgun back across his shoulder, he stumped back to the adobe. The fascinated audience finally succumbed to all-out hilarity.

Some time passed before the travellers got themselves settled to sleep again.

'We've spoiled some of Black Dog's medicine fer him,' Spragg had said with satisfaction. 'But I'll bet my ma's nightgown that he weren't along on that raid. He'll say as it was those young bucks that done had the bad medicine, and how the others got to foller him.'

Cullen spoke quietly. 'The best way for Black Dog to prove up on his boast is for him to lead a victory. And I reckon we look like a plumb good target for him.' It took all of his self-control not to look accusingly at Wybourn.

Right on cue, the businessman spoke. 'Those Comanches can't be trusted, except to do harm.' He flicked the dishevelled grey forelock back off his face. 'This isn't their world any longer.'

'I reckon they'd give you a fight about that,' Spragg said.

'They're going to lose,' Wybourn prophesied. 'The world's moving fast now and only those who can change their ways and work hard are going to make anything of it. You have to grab chance when you can,' he added passionately.

'We sure have,' Cullen agreed.

The two men locked gazes for a moment. Wybourn frowned slightly and seemed to be on the verge of asking a question. Cullen gazed back confidently.

'We'd be best getting some rest,' Hyde interrupted. 'Not stand here talking like the Ladies' Shakespeare Reading Circle.' As he had intended, the tension broke at once. In the general bustle, he managed a private word with Cullen.

'Don't go starting anything out here on the trail,' he said softly. 'We may yet need to fight together again before we can start fighting amongst ourselves.'

'Mmmm.' Tense as he was, Cullen could see the sense in Hyde's remark. Besides, it was another good reason for keeping the news about the receipt for the guns to himself.

He slept well for the rest of the night.

6

In spite of the broken night's sleep, Spragg got everyone up early.

'I ain't never been late with the stage yet, an' I shore ain't gonna be startin' now,' he grumbled. All the time as he complained, his rough hands were gently settling harness, soothing horses and rubbing velvet muzzles as he got the team ready. 'You's meant to be havin' a rest today. I don't like asking you cow-hocked mustangs to haul this bunch of wuthless no-goods about, but we ain't got no choice, see? We'll git 'em to El Paso on time, Injuns or no Injuns, eh?'

As soon as the last spoonful of reheated beans had been swallowed, Spragg was bustling them on their way and threatening to leave anyone who wasn't in the wagon when he was ready to go.

'You ain't no fool in a fight,' he told Cullen while glancing sideways at Robinson. 'You kin watch aside of me.'

So the salesman sat alongside the leathery driver on the box. Robinson and Jefferson were at the back, keeping rear watch. Wybourn was in the middle and Mary and Don sat at the front.

The team were slower now. Spragg held them to a steady jog, speaking to his horses frequently. 'Get along there, Raven. Ain't no use you dawdling, you's gonna get there same time's the rest of us.' He flicked the lash just above the grey horse's ears.

Cullen let the stream of words flow past unheeded. He glanced now and again at Hyde, who was riding alongside. Most of the time, his eyes were scanning for ambush. They were travelling through low mountains, mostly going uphill. Sheer rock faces soared upwards, crowned with cedars and scrubby oaks. The trail itself was shaded here and there by pecan trees, walnuts and cypresses. It was beautiful, striking country that the travellers watched with endless suspicion.

'I haven't seen any hint of Indian presence all morning,' Robinson said after a long silence. 'That means they're not following any more, yeah?'

'Nope,' Cullen answered. 'The time to start worrying is when you stop seeing Comanches.' Robinson didn't bother to answer.

Towards noon, the trail curved up more steeply than before. The horses leaned into their harnesses. Patches of sweat on their coats began to rub into foam. Spragg spoke to them gently, urging them on.

'When we stops at noon, I aim on giving them some of that grain we be carrying to El Paso,' he said.

Cullen nodded. 'If we make it that far,' he said quietly. Behind him, Mary Schmidt turned on the hard wooden bench. 'Where are we now?' she asked.

'This is Finlay Pass.' Spragg said. He was leaning forward on the box, as if trying to ease the weight his team were pulling. 'Once we reach the summit, we'll be rolling down to the Rio Grande. Trail follers alongside of that, rest of the way.'

'This is an ideal place for an ambush,' Wyburn said clearly from his seat within the wagon.

Don glanced anxiously at his wife, more than a little scared himself. She smiled back radiantly.

'I'm not scared,' she told him. 'Because I've got you to look after me.' Don smiled back, touched and rather alarmed at her faith in him.

On the box, Cullen asked Spragg, 'You know this trail better'n any of us,' he said. 'Do you think Black Dog'll jump us here?'

Whiskers Spragg chewed on his tobacco as he thought. Finally, he nodded. 'A mite further up'd be best. Even iffen we make the top, there's a mighty sharp turn in the trail on the far side.'

Now that he had been reminded,

Cullen recalled the hazard. The trail wound past a huge outcrop from the canyon wall. It curved at first, then made a right-angled bend, with a sharp drop to the valley floor below.

Cullen's attention was drawn to the team as one of the horses slipped on loose stones. The bay gelding lurched forward in its harness, pulling its partner off balance.

'Ease up there, Solly,' Spragg called. His leathery hands played expertly with the lines, slowing the lead horses, supporting the struggling one and reasuring the wheelers. The old-timer's blue eyes were fixed on his team as they hauled the wagon up the rough trail.

As Solly, the bay, recovered itself a Comanche brave broke from cover on the other side of the narrow valley. The young warrior screamed out his war cry as he kicked his mustang into a wild gallop, firing his Yellowboy repeater as he came. At that speed and distance, he stood no chance of making a hit. Even as other Indians broke cover, their ambush set off too soon, Hyde halted his mount. The rifle flowed smoothly to his shoulder. He sighted and fired almost before it stopped moving. The reckless brave tumbled backwards off his mustang and rolled in the dirt.

'Yeeaahh!' Spragg's wild cry rang out. He shook the leather lines and cracked his whip in the air. His team renewed their efforts, hooves scrabbling on the stony ground as they hauled the wagon up the slope to the top of the pass. On the back, Robinson grabbed the wagon frame with one hand and raised the pistol that Hyde had loaned him.

'Look at that!' he exclaimed, his eyes alight with admiration and excitement.

Over twenty Comanche warriors were spilling from ambush, racing their horses after the fleeing wagon. They weren't decorated with feathers, or wearing beautifully beaded costumes, but Robinson wasn't disappointed with them. Even with the dust flying up from their horses' hooves, he could see that all the warriors were wearing paint and one had a buffalo-horn headdress. Some carried shields with medicine designs, or trailing feathers. Two carried lances with deadly, steel-tipped points.

'Oh my,' the young Easterner breathed. Even the crackle of gunfire couldn't dampen his enthusiasm. Beside him, Jefferson held tight to the long-handled axe and muttered prayers under his breath.

Up front, Cullen had Spragg's shot-gun ready for action. It was a deadly weapon, but most effective at closer ranges. He was mighty grateful that the Comanches were closing in for hand to hand combat instead of using their rifles.

'Even the herd boys've got repeaters,' he yelled above the noise.

Spragg didn't answer; he was too busy driving the wagon. The horses responded to his calls and curses, plunging into a gallop. He kept them in the middle of the trail, sparing no time to watch the Comanches closing in. Beside him, Cullen was measuring speed and distance. The wagon should just reach the narrow turn on the trail before the Indians caught up. They would be no safer on the other side of the pass, but at least the team would be hauling the wagon downhill. There wasn't much room to spare on either side of the wagon, which would force the Comanches to approach in narrow file.

Cullen braced his feet against the front boot to keep himself on the driver's box as the wagon bounced furiously over the dirt trail. Mary's chickens squawked and cackled indignantly as their coop bounced against the side.

Hyde's mount shifted restlessly as bullets sprayed from his rifle. The wagon was fleeing up the trail but Hyde chose to stay in place for better shooting while he had the chance. The Indians were bunched together as they broke from cover. He glimpsed a couple sliding sideways, saw one fall for certain, and heard a horse scream in pain. A black mustang fell at full gallop. Its stocky rider landed on his feet, ran a couple of steps, then swung himself up behind a companion as another horse thundered past. Hyde fired a dozen shots in as many seconds. Most hit home somewhere; gunsmoke and flying dust made it impossible for him to see exactly.

Then the Comanches were too close for safety. Shoving the rifle into its boot with his right hand, he snatched up the reins with the other and swung his horse around. The chestnut was more than ready to go. It bounded straight into a gallop, head stretched low as it chased the fleeing wagon. Hyde sat easily in the deep saddle; blood from his earlier injury was soaking into the sleeve of his black jacket. He gritted his teeth and urged his horse on.

'Look at that! That's courage!' Robinson exclaimed as he watched Hyde make his stand.

'Mister Hyde's surely gonna git shot,' Jefferson answered more practically.

'We'll give him covering fire, yeah?' Robinson still had one of Hyde's matched revolvers. He fired it twice into the mob of Indians without any apparent effect.

There weren't enough guns in the party to spare one for Jefferson, even if the black man had wanted one. He hung on to the axe, ready to use it if a target came close enough. Inside the wagon, Wybourn had used his pocket-knife to slash away one of the canvas side-curtains. With that out of the way, he also started shooting. A pony stumbled; its rider hung on with amazing skill, hauling it up again only to find his mount completely lame. The Comanche bounded off and gave chase on foot. His injured pony limped back to the shelter of some trees.

Up front, Mary Schmidt was leaning out over the box, peering between Cullen and Spragg. Don was beside her, trying to persuade his wife to move to a safer position. Mary encouraged the team horses on with shouts and yells, completely ignoring her husband. The alarmed chickens added their noise to the brew of thundering hooves, rattling wagon and gunfire. Cullen twisted sideways on the box, getting aim on an ambitious Comanche who had cut across at an angle and was racing his mount up the steep slope beside the trail. The shotgun bellowed and the Comanche screamed, his naked chest riddled with shot.

'Get him!' Mary yelled. 'Give him the other barrel!'

The Comanche was dying, but he aimed to make it a glorious death. He screamed his war-cry, blood spitting from his mouth, and urged his pony closer. It cleared the top of the slope, lunging forward across the flatter trail. The Comanche raised his club, steering his pony closer to the box.

'Go on!' Mary screamed. 'Don't wait!'

The Comanche was almost within

arm's reach when Cullen fired again. The shot shredded the Indian's torso, turning it to bloody pulp. His pony veered away from the crash and flame, sending its rider over its shoulder. He fell and bounced down the slope, dead before he reached the bottom. Cullen thrust the shotgun at Don, behind him.

'Reload that.'

The next moment he was almost catapulted off his seat as Spragg hauled his galloping team down to a walking pace.

The horses snorted, their sides heaving in the harnesses.

'Keep going,' Don exclaimed, clutching the shotgun. 'They're almost here!' He peered nervously around.

Cullen said nothing as he unholstered his gun, he knew what Spragg was doing.

They were approaching the sharp turn in the trail. The horses jogged nervously, still unsettled, as they reached the first part of the turn.

'What are you doing?' Mary asked anxiously. She clutched Cullen's arm, frightened but sensible enough not to distract Spragg as he handled the reins.

'Watch,' Cullen told her.

The curve in the trail was gentle at first, no hazard to the wagon, but enough to prevent them from seeing what lay around the corner. The wild screams of the Comanches grew rapidly closer as Spragg held his team to a walk. Gunfire crackled out again, almost drowning Spragg's voice as he spoke to the horses. As they rounded the bend, the passengers saw the massive outcropping that Spragg had mentioned earlier.

The slope on the right of the trail fell away dramatically. Before them opened a view into a wider, deeper canyon. The trail ran high along one side, gradually making its way down to the wide canyon floor. Wind-carved walls of red-and buff-striped stone enclosed the canyon, sheltering the lush country at the bottom. It was a stunning view, but at that moment, no one paid it a second thought. Here the trail made its sharp turn.

Spragg concentrated on his team, even forgetting to chew the lump of tobacco in his cheek. The horses were still blowing and excited from the noise behind them and their wild gallop.

'Easy now, Betty. Jest you tek it slow.'

The bay mare threw her head up and down restlessly, but she obeyed the familiar touch on the reins. She moved with delicate steps on the inside of the turn, while the gelding to her outside moved faster. Cullen spared a moment to glance down the hundred-yard drop just a couple of feet from the wagon's right wheels.

'Move over that way,' he ordered, gesturing to the left. Mary and Don did as they were told.

'Come on, come on, come on,' Don muttered steadily.

'The shotgun,' Mary reminded him. The young farmer stared blankly

at her for a moment, before understanding. Don broke open the shotgun
and fumbled out the spent shells in
order to reload it.

The first two horses were out of sight
around the turn. The next pair swung
out a little wider. The outer wheels
of the wagon edged closer to the
drop. Behind them, the Comanches
had almost caught up. Spragg made no
attempt to hurry, but coaxed his team
steadily around the corner. His hands
manipulated the leather lines, daintily
controlling each pair of horses. They
moved forward with smooth precision,
as if he had been driving a team
of schooled carriage-horses, not six
Western mustangs.

The passengers at the back of the
wagon couldn't see the dangers of
the trail ahead; what they would see
was the band of Comanche warriors
getting closer by the second. Hyde
had caught up with the wagon and
rode close by the rear wheel. His
arm throbbed steadily as the bullet

wound reopened from his exertions. Trusting his horse to stay away from the drop, he twisted in the saddle to shoot the Comanches. Inside the wagon, Robinson and Wybourn were doing the same. Their gunfire crackled at irregular intervals but the jogging of the wagon made it hard to aim accurately.

'Which one's Black Dog?' Robinson yelled over the noise. He was crouching behind the tail-gate, clutching the Colt, two-handed. Hyde flinched as a bullet tore through his black Stetson. Few of the Comanches were firing guns, preferring hand to hand combat. Those who were shooting were doing so from their running ponies, using new, unfamiliar weapons. Even so, at this range they wouldn't keep missing for ever.

Hyde picked a target and fired. A stout warrior with flashes of blue paint down his chest was pitched over the back of his mount and vanished beneath the pounding hooves of the others.

Wybourn answered the question. 'The buck on the sorrel paint,' he said with confidence.

Black Dog was a barrel-chested man, heavy and powerful but graceful in the way he rode his tall horse. Only the elaborate beading on his moccasins and the quality of his mount showed him to be the leader of the group. As an established warrior, he could afford to let his followers ride ahead to count coup and gain prizes. Warlike and competitive as Comanches were, a warrior gained respect for his generosity and charity, and Black Dog was determined to live up to the highest standards of his people. He held his new repeater ready for action and let his wild band of warriors charge after the slow wagon.

Wybourn recognized the Comanche leader even through all the dust. He didn't aim at him though; instead, he carefully lined on one of the lance-carrying bucks. As the wagon slowly rounded the sharp turn in the trail, the Comanches' screams rose to a new pitch of excitement. Their ponies closed with every stride until only a few paces separated them from the whites.

The two lance-carriers were slightly ahead of the mob. They both held their long weapons low, preferring an underarm thrust. Robinson shot at one of the horses, reluctant to fire deliberately on a man he could see clearly. The pony stumbled and fell with a scream of agony. Its rider landed on his feet, lance in hand, and ran on with barely a pause.

Wybourn knew Comanches better than the Easterner. He knew the warrior who carried a lance had sworn to fight or die without retreating; he shot to kill the man. His victim jerked and grabbed for his pony's mane, clinging on with desperate skill. The pony fell back among the mob where Wybourn could no longer see him clearly. The injured warrior raised his lance again and urged his pony forward.

Robinson downed another horse

before the Colt's hammer clicked on to an empty chamber. He gaped at the gun for a moment, before sensibly ducking below the tail-gate. The Comanches were making no attempt to slow as they reached the wagon. Hyde's horse backed and twirled restlessly as the whooping mob closed in. Its hooves kicked stones off the edge of the trail and into free air. Hyde had no time to take a shot; he needed both hands on the reins as his frightened horse pirouetted on the edge of the drop.

'Get down!' The yell came from Don Schmidt.

Robinson half glanced over his shoulder, saw the young farmer pointing the shotgun back along the wagon, and flattened himself to the wagon floor beside Jefferson, grabbing Wybourn's sleeve to pull him down too. The shotgun boomed, spraying lead and hot air over their heads. Jefferson cursed but the words were lost in the noise. The long gun boomed a second time. Only then did anyone dare to look up.

7

The leading Comanches had fallen back a few strides. As Wybourn lifted his Colt to fire again, the wagon suddenly lurched into a gallop. They had rounded the tight corner, the mob of Comanches following hard. Hyde had got his prancing horse over to the inside of the trail, well away from the long drop.

'Here!' He tossed his Winchester into the back of the wagon. With the enemy so close behind on a narrow trail, the rifle was too cumbersome, even if his injured arm hadn't been hurting. Jefferson caught it and promptly handed it over to Robinson.

'Tuck it tight to your shoulder,' Wybourn advised. He had crouched low and was reloading his Navy Colt. Even though the wagon was jouncing all over the place, he managed the fiddly job competently.

Then the first Comanches were upon them. One jumped from his pony to the back of the wagon. He clung to the tail-gate with one hand and swung his hatchet at Robinson with the other. The startled newspaperman had a vivid impression of coppery skin, yellow paint and pure, primitive violence. Robinson jerked back from the sudden movement and struck out instinctively. The hatchet sliced past the front of his grey shirt as Robinson thumped the Comanche with his Winchester's barrel. The sight on the end of the rifle cut the Indian's cheek and distracted him for a vital moment. Jefferson lunged up from his place on the wagon floor and swung his long axe with great precision. The blade chopped deep into the base of the Comanche's neck. Blood squirted out before the mortally wounded man fell from the back of the bouncing wagon.

'Excellent,' Wybourn said briefly. He rose up firing as another Indian attempted to board the wagon. The brave jerked as the bullet hit him, inadvertently swerving his galloping horse to the right. Its hooves scrabbled briefly on the edge of the trail before the earth crumbled under it. Man and horse fell together. Others were already pushing past the wagon. The team horses were giving their best, but with the weight they were pulling, they never stood a chance of outrunning the fresher Indian ponies. The trail was growing broader as it descended from the pass. Passing the racing wagon was dangerous, but the Comanches were the finest riders of all the horse Indians.

'There's two coming up,' Mary called, glimpsing them through the curtain that Wybourn had cut open. She was sitting tight behind the driver's box.

Cullen twisted, thumbing back the hammer of his short revolver. Beside him, Spragg was cursing steadily as he urged his team on.

'Goddamn Indjuns. Makin' me run

the team into the ground. I ain't gonna let them hold up the stage none. I never been late yet an' I sure as sin don't mean to start now.'

Cullen fired his first shot as the wagon bounced over a rock. His shot went into the air. The young Comanche pulling alongside swung his club, forcing the salesman to duck. Another Indian was right behind the first, knife in hand.

Mary was desperate to help. Glancing around, she realized that Spragg wasn't using the long whip, preferring to keep both hands on the reins as the team raced down the slanting trail. Seizing the leather bullwhip, Mary leaned across the wagon, yelling at the top of her voice.

'Get out of here!' she screamed, not really thinking about what she was saying. She tried to swing the lash round but there wasn't room from her position inside the wagon.

Cullen was in trouble, but he kept his head. The last jolt of the wagon

163

had thrown him forward in the box, and off balance. He was hanging on to the back of the seat with his left hand, trying to get a shot at the Comanche. Although the range was so close, he hadn't done more than graze the buck's stomach. He dodged again as the club swung, feeling it brush his clothing. His short gun was out of line again. The wagon jolted, tipping Cullen closer to the Comanche. He gritted his teeth and clung on for dear life, knowing he had to get a clear shot, no matter what the risk. The Comanche struck again, bringing his stone-headed club around with brutal force. Cullen got off a single shot and knew he'd got the Comanche, just before the club smashed into his chest. The salesman felt pain, feeling ribs crack under the impact. He barely saw the Comanche slide sideways on his horse and fall back.

The second Comanche saw his chance and started his attack.

'Leave him alone!' Mary yelled,

leaning out to swing the whip. She was clumsy with the long, heavy leather. Instead of hitting the Indian, the lash struck his pony across the face. The startled mount skidded and stumbled, throwing its rider as it fell to its knees and rolled down the trail. The Comanche twisted like a cat and landed on his feet, his momentum carrying him forward at a run. He had taken just two strides when the chicken-coop tied to the side of the wagon smashed into his back and knocked him over. He rolled once and slipped over the edge of the trail, vanishing with a scream.

No one on the wagon saw him go. The wagon bounced over a rock, throwing everyone forward. Cullen was bashed against the front of the box, gasping breathlessly at the pain in his ribs. He was too dazed to grab on to anything and went sliding dangerously forward. Mary saw him toppling off the seat and dropped the whip to grab the back of his shirt. She got a good hold, but the salesman was a solidly built man, and she was already leaning out further than was safe.

'Don!' Mary screamed for her husband as Cullen's weight dragged her forwards. She clung on to him none the less, trying to brace herself, but her long skirts hampered her efforts. Cullen was scrabbling for a hold but the endless jerking and jouncing of the wagon kept him off balance.

Don Schmidt heard his wife's cry for help and promptly abandoned all other actions. Dropping the shotgun, he scrambled over the seat and the goods stored on the floor. His left hand closed on Mary's hoops and skirts, halting her slide forward. The next moment Don had his right arm around her waist. He hauled his wife back into safety.

'Here.' Once Mary was safe, he reached round her to take Cullen's arm. Between them, they got him back on the box seat.

'Are you hurt?' Mary asked anxiously. Her sweet rosebud mouth was pursed becomingly.

'Not to worry about,' Cullen answered, pressing one hand carefully over his ribs.

Don Schmidt swelled up with pride at his wife's courage. Remembering the shotgun, he picked it up and swung around to look for more enemies. He vowed that when they reached El Paso, he would buy himself both a shotgun and a revolver and learn to be good with each. Never again would he have to rely on others to protect his brave wife.

The rear of the wagon was better defended. Hyde and Wybourn were both skilled with their guns. Robinson was clumsy with the rifle, but the Comanches were right behind the wagon and riding in a bunch on the narrow trail; even the newspaperman couldn't help hitting some targets. One Comanche started shooting back, tearing splinters from the frame supporting the canvas curtains. He immediately made himself a target. Two bullets struck him in the chest, knocking him backwards off his racing mount.

As suddenly as the attack had come, it began to wither away. Only the injured lance-carrier pressed his attack home.

Bursting through the bunch, he drove straight for Hyde. The gunman was out of bullets and had nowhere to run; he was trapped behind the wagon on the narrow trail. As the steel-tipped lance was thrust towards him, he grabbed his saddle horn and swung sideways. The lance head grazed painfully over his leg and tore his jacket. From the back of the wagon, Wybourn and Robinson both fired. The Comanche died instantly, dropping limply from his pony. The deadly lance clattered on to the dirt trail. Hyde struggled ungracefully back into his saddle. He was gasping for breath and a little dizzy, and kept hold of the pommel as his horse thundered along. Blood from his arm-wound had trickled down his sleeve on to his hand.

One of the Comanches leaned down from his bounding pony to scoop up the body of the lance-carrier. He pulled off the tricky stunt with an ease that drew a gasp of admiration from Robinson. Then the warriors were turning, letting the wagon go. All the survivors were carrying injured or dead braves with them as they turned to race back over the pass.

Don Schmidt gave a whoop of excitement. 'We did it! We saw 'em off!'

Wybourn pushed two more rounds into his revolver, watching steadily to make sure it wasn't a trick from the Comanches. Beside him, Robinson held the rifle ready.

'Would they really retreat?' he asked. 'I understood that most Indian warriors aimed to die gloriously in combat, yeah?'

'They reckon it's a good way to die,'

Wybourn told him. 'But they also got families to feed.'

The last Comanche vanished from sight. Wybourn carefully lowered the hammer on his gun and called an all-clear to Spragg.

With the excitement over, Robinson was checking on his fellow-passengers. Jefferson was wiping blood from the blade of the axe. Hyde was riding close up behind the wagon.

'Why, I believe we made it all right,' the Southerner remarked.

Robinson noticed the blood on the other man's hand. 'Say, you're hurt, yeah?' He glanced back and saw Cullen had one hand pressed against his ribs. 'We should stop somewhere and effect some first aid.'

'This isn't the place yet,' Wybourn said calmly. He smoothed his forelock back into place. 'Somewhere down in the canyon would be better.'

Spragg had already slowed the team from their gallop. His hands were light on the reins as he eased them back to a steady jog. The old-timer mumbled to himself at the state of his horses, and the foamy sweat dripping off them.

'Goddam redskins ain't got nothin' better to do than to chase my hosses ragged. These ain't even riding hosses nohow.'

When they reached the canyon floor, he drove along to a wide spot near the river before halting. As soon as the weary horses stopped, he bellowed for Jefferson and Robinson to come help him. Both went to unharness the team, Robinson voicing his thoughts even as he worked buckles loose.

'Shouldn't we be helping Cullen and Hyde?' he asked, unhooking traces from the bay mare's collar.

'This team still got to get us to El Paso,' Spragg told him. 'There's Comanche, Yaqui an' plenty o' mean greaser *bandidos* runnin' in this stretch o' country. Any o' them takes a fancy to our hosses an' guns, we're all gonna need this team to run again. Team allus gets fixed up first.'

'Yuh goin' to give the hawses that grain we's carrying?' Jefferson reminded the old-timer.

'Sure.' Spragg led a pair of horses into the shallow river. He stood calf-deep in the swirling, cool water as the horses drank. As the brown gelding gulped noisily, Spragg examined the horse's legs. Jefferson was doing the same with the sorrel mare. The two men exchanged opinions with a glance.

'We ain't gonna make it today,' Spragg announced.

'What, to El Paso?' Robinson asked.

Jefferson poured hatfuls of cold river water over the sorrel's legs to stop swelling and stiffness forming after the hard run. Spragg watched with approval.

'S'right,' he told Robinson. 'Hosses ain't got the pull left in them. We'll night up someplace around Acala. Make an easy run into town termorrer mornin'.'

Back at the wagon, Mary Schmidt was helping Cullen. She had helped him to strip off jacket and shirt and was peering at the dark bruise forming on his ribs.

'That's going to be mighty sore,' she told him sympathetically. 'But I've got some witch hazel.' She climbed inside the wagon and fetched a shallow square box of polished wood that he hadn't noticed before. She opened it to reveal row upon row of tiny, cork-stoppered bottles. Mary took one, without even needing to check the label, shook it briskly and poured some of its contents on to a white cloth. This, she pressed against Cullen's bare chest.

'Does that help?' she asked.

'Er . . . sure.' It was certainly distracting. 'I never saw a medicine box like that before,' Cullen said, glancing around to see whether Don Schmidt was watching them.

'Oh, it's my mother's,' Mary answered. 'She said I'd need it more out on the frontier than she would back to home.'

'I guess she was right.' Cullen relaxed

and started to enjoy the experience.

Wybourn had built a fire and was boiling water.

'You making coffee?' Don asked, rather surprised by this behaviour. He was still carrying Spragg's shotgun, pretending to himself that they might be ambushed again. Wybourn was equally surprised by the ignorant question.

'I'm cleaning my guns,' he said, impatiently shaking the grey forelock back off his face. 'The barrels get plumb fouled with gunpowder after a long fight.' As he spoke, he unrolled the kit containing his cleaning tools. 'A man can't risk having a gun that won't fire well; not if he aims to protect himself.'

'I see.' Don crouched near the little fire. 'Should I clean this shotgun then?'

Wybourn looked up from his work. 'I guess so.' He hesitated a moment before bowing to the inevitable. 'I'll show you how, then. If a man's gonna do a thing, he should learn to do it right. There's no place for folks who're too weak to cope on their own.'

Hyde unsaddled, watered and rubbed down his horse before thinking of himself. He moved slowly, a little dizzy, but didn't leave the liver chestnut until it was nuzzling up a hatful of grain from the sack that Spragg had opened. By that time, the blood on his hand and arm had dried and cracked into stiff flakes. Robinson saw Hyde struggling to remove his jacket and came over to help.

'We had better wash that off in the river, yeah?' he remarked, folding the black jacket neatly before putting it down.

'You done got some blood on your face,' Hyde told him, bending over to sluice water over his arm.

Surprised, Robinson rubbed his hand over his face and felt the splashes of blood crusted there. 'Oh, I remember.' He thought of the Indian that Jefferson had killed with the axe, then thought about the ones he had shot at himself. 'Lots of those Comanche died.'

'We sure didn't ask them to attack us.' Hyde understood what the Easterner was thinking and was curious to see how Robinson would react.

The newspaperman leaned over the river-bank to splash water on his face. He rubbed away the dried blood.

'No, of course not. I'm sure I killed some of them, but they were trying to kill me, weren't they?' There was a slightly pleading note in Robinson's voice.

'You have any doubt about that?' Hyde drawled as he unwound the blood-soaked bandage from his arm.

Robinson shook his head without needing to think about it. He smiled wryly. 'I never imagined I would take a man's life, but if I hadn't defended myself, they would have killed me.'

'That's the paradox,' Hyde agreed. He sat back on the grass, inspecting the wound. It seemed to have stopped bleeding but the scab was still soft. The graze on his leg would need some attention, but was a minor hurt.

'I didn't panic though.'

Hyde looked up, hearing the pride in Robinson's voice.

'It was the first real military action I have been engaged in, yeah? And I didn't panic.' Robinson started to grin.

'You didn't exactly panic when you shot yourself a Comanche in the dark last night,' Hyde reminded him.

'True.' Robinson thought for a moment. 'But I couldn't really see him. Today they were close enough that I could see them as individuals, as men, not just targets.'

'I guess you're learning about living in the wild, woolly West,' Hyde drawled.

Robinson's face lit up. 'Just think what a letter this will make. The circulation's just bound to go up.' He bounced energetically to his feet. 'I'll go see about fetching some bandages to fix your arm, yeah?'

'Thanks.'

Robinson took one long stride before

pausing and glancing back. 'If I hadn't killed those men, people would have been hurt?'

Hyde nodded.

Robinson nodded slowly to himself, then strode quickly over to the wagon. Mary gave him a couple of linen bandages.

'I'll start fixing some lunch now those two have finished with the kettle,' she told him, pointing at Wybourn and her husband.

Robinson hadn't noticed the lesson on gun care. On his way back to Hyde, he detoured closer to the fire and was so busy eavesdropping that he almost fell over his own feet. Mary giggled.

'I'll go start some coffee,' she said to Cullen.

'Thank you. You're a for-real lady.' He winked saucily at her and was rewarded by a smile.

Cullen sat on the lowered tail-gate of the wagon for a while. Mary was soon engrossed in her cooking. The salesman took a good look around the camp, seeing that the others were all engaged in activity. When no one was looking his way, he simply vanished back into the wagon. A deft twist of his penknife blade opened the lock on Wybourn's bag and he recommenced the search that Hyde had interrupted the day before.

This time Cullen opened the other compartment and felt around inside. He could feel good linen shirts and a starched collar. Tucked in a corner were socks. Cullen got his fingers right into the corners, getting the inevitable dust and bits jammed under his short fingernails as he felt about for hidden pockets. His pulse jumped as his fingertips pushed into a slit at the bottom of the dividing flap. Holding his breath, he searched deeper still. The slit gave a little, but then he encountered the soft brush of fabric. The slit was nothing more than a gap in the bottom of the leather that divided the two sections of the valise.

'Damn!' Cullen muttered viciously.

Pulling his fingers back he decided to take out the leather toilet bag and search that.

The first he knew of Wybourn's presence was a heavy blow on the ear.

8

The blow almost knocked Cullen off the wagon bench. He dropped Wybourn's valise, shaking his hand clear of the restricting object. Wybourn didn't give him a chance to recover but struck again. He aimed low, deliberately punching Cullen in his injured ribs. Cullen gave a squeaking gasp and landed on his back, trapped awkwardly between the benches and all the goods on the floor of the wagon.

'What in hell're you doing, you stinking thief you?' Wybourn hissed.

Cullen couldn't answer; he was white in the face with pain from his cracked ribs.

'I done got you red-handed.' Wybourn flicked back his stray forelock of hair as he glared down at the other man.

'And you,' Cullen gasped.

Wybourn frowned at that, his black

brows drawing together. The pause gave Cullen a few more moments to gather his wits.

'You were stealing my valise,' Wybourn said. 'I'll see that you get handed over to the sheriff in El Paso.'

Cullen shook his head. 'I was looking for what you stole from me.' He grabbed the edge of a bench and struggled to sit up. Stabs of pain shot through his chest but he grimly ignored them.

'Your brain's addled,' Wybourn told him. 'Why should I want to steal any of your goods?'

Cullen couldn't take the time to think things through; he had to get this sorted before anyone else came along and explanations had to be made.

'You stole a map from my poppa.' Cullen tried to speak evenly but there was a bitterness he couldn't quite hide. 'My poppa was Rory Williams, and you two rode together in the War. I wrote you and you denied it.'

Understanding lit up Wybourn's face.

'Williams's son. I was sure I knew you from someplace.' He looked more critically at the younger man. 'You're some heavier than your pa though.'

Cullen didn't deign to answer that particular comment. 'You took his map. That's why you've been setting up in El Paso.' The words tumbled out faster and faster. 'I've been trailing you. I know about your shares in the bank and your hunting trips out. You've been searching for the silver my poppa found. It's mine! That silver belongs to my family!'

'It belongs to me now,' Wybourn retorted unexpectedly. 'I've got that lode just about ready to pay out. It's going to keep me comfortable for the rest of my life.'

'What about my momma and my sisters?' Cullen said indignantly. 'If I had that mine they wouldn't need to work.'

'You can find your own damn mine. You're young, you've got plenty of time to make yourself a good living.

I worked damn hard all my life and I lost 'most all of it in the War. When I found that map on Williams's body, I took it as my reward for tryin' to save his life. That silver mine's my chance to live in decent comfort the rest of my life and I sure intend to take it.'

'You won't find it so comfortable in prison,' Cullen threatened.

Wybourn glared defiantly at him. 'How're you gonna prove anything? Your pa never registered his claim.'

'I wasn't thinking of the mine. I was thinking about you selling repeaters to the Comanches.'

Wybourn simply said, 'That ain't gonna hold up in court.'

'Oh it will. Look in your hat.'

The businessman stared suspiciously at him.

Cullen grinned. 'That receipt for thirty Winchester repeaters you were hiding. I got that now.'

'It isn't illegal to buy repeaters,' Wybourn said stiffly.

'Giving them to wild Comanches is.'

'That's plumb impossible to prove.'

'You got any proof of what you did with thirty repeating rifles? We've got proof enough that Black Dog and his bucks've got repeaters. You think any Western jury's gonna let you go?'

'They'd need better proof,' Wybourn said stubbornly. His narrow eyes betrayed him, though. He knew perfectly well how Westerners would feel about anyone reasonably suspected of gun-running to bad Indians.

Cullen pressed the point home. 'I bet ol' Spragg wouldn't bother even wasting time with a trial. If he knew you'd given Black Dog those Winchesters, he'd string you up here and now.'

'The Easterners wouldn't let him.'

'They wouldn't be able to stop him.' It was no more than the plain truth.

Cullen shifted position again, sitting on the middle wagon bench. He took the time to tuck his shirt back into his waistband.

'I want that map back,' he said. 'That silver belongs to me.'

'It's my pension,' Wybourn repeated.

'You can keep any you've already got from it. When we get to El Paso, I'll give you the receipt back, and you turn the map over to me. A straight swap, and silence from us both.'

'No.'

'I'll get you strung up for selling guns to Indians. Even if you do stay out of jail, you'll be ruined.'

'All right. You got your deal.' Wybourn glared at him.

'I want your word on it,' Cullen insisted, his face cold.

Wybourn smiled wryly. 'You reckon I stick to my word?'

'Poppa reckoned you were a friend. I'll trust his judgement.'

'Your pa was a fine man,' Wybourn said suddenly. 'I tried to save him.'

'I know.'

'You got a deal.' Wybourn glared at him. 'Now get out. If you let out a word about the repeaters, you'll never see so much as an ounce of silver from that mine.'

'When I aim to do something, I see it through.'

With that Cullen climbed from the wagon, leaving Wybourn to tidy the contents of his valise and scowl darkly at his thoughts.

★ ★ ★

The travellers rested for an hour before harnessing the horses and pressing on. In spite of his conscience being in a whirl over shooting Comanches, Robinson was delighted to be asked to sit alongside Spragg. He scrambled eagerly on to the box and perched there, holding Hyde's Winchester. He was also delighted to find there was plenty of room for his long legs. Mary Schmidt nagged Hyde about resting his wounded arm properly, until he gave in with a sudden smile and agreed to ride in the wagon. Don took his riding horse and the shotgun. He wasn't a polished rider but the hard run earlier had left the liver chestnut too leg-weary to play up. Cullen travelled propped against the sacks of letters. He was in a cheerful mood and kept the other passengers entertained with a constant flow of stories and jokes. Wybourn sat in his place at the rear of the wagon, and moodily smoked his expensive cigars.

The team plodded steadily onwards. As the afternoon wore on, even Cullen's cheerful mood faded away. The only sounds were the plod of hooves in the dusty trail, the creaking of the wagon and Jefferson singing hymns under his breath.

'Is Black Dog likely to attack again?' Mary's question broke the uneasy silence.

'Most likely not,' Cullen answered confidently. 'The attack was plumb bad for him. His medicine went real sour.'

'What does 'medicine' mean exactly?' Robinson asked. 'I keep hearing the expression, yeah, but I'll have to put a clear explanation into my letters so my readers will understand.'

Spragg spoke up. 'It's a Comanche's

magical power an' Black Dog reckons he's got a whole heap of it. The other bucks foller him 'cause he's got power to gain coups an' prizes fer 'em all.' A spurt of tobacco juice hit a juniper bush. 'With us downin' so many of 'em, the others'll reckon as how his medicine done turned bad. They won't foller him so eagerly next time.'

'So, his failure means losing the loyalty of his men, yeah?' Robinson asked.

'They ain't really his men,' Spragg said, but was interrupted by the discussion inside the wagon.

'Why sure Comanches are brave, but I declare they don't know how to be loyal like white folks,' Hyde announced. 'Or like slaves do,' he added to Jefferson.

'Indians got more sense than to stick with a losing side,' Wybourn said sharply.

'They rescued their friends though,' Mary pointed out.

'Sure, that's a personal thing and

mighty fine. But Comanches don't understand loyalty to abstracts, like a cause,' Hyde drawled.

'A man who does his best to survive is no fool,' Wybourn shot back, stabbing the air with his cigar. 'I spent five years fighting for the goddamn Confederacy and it got me nothing but hungry, broke and injured. And look where the Noble Cause got you,' he said to Hyde with bitter sarcasm. 'You lost your plantation, your wealth and your slaves. You're nothing but a professional gunman now. That's hardly a gentleman's work.'

There was no warning; Hyde simply launched himself across the crowded wagon and slammed into Wybourn. He knocked the businessman back into the tail-gate, bringing a cry of pain. The cigar dropped to the floor of the wagon and smouldered. Hyde slammed punches into the businessman's face. Jefferson snatched up the burning cigar and stubbed it out, taking a quick puff first.

'Stop it!' Mary shrieked.

Cullen just watched, unwilling to intervene. Robinson screwed himself around on the box, wishing he was inside where the others were. Spragg busied himself with the reins, speaking to his horses to soothe them as the wagon bounced around. It was Jefferson who seized Hyde's shoulders and pulled him away.

'Doan' yuh be gettin' yoself inner trouble wit' him now, suh,' The black man advised.

'You-all heard what he said about the Confederacy,' Hyde retorted, shaking himself free. His grey eyes glittered as he glanced defiantly at the others in the wagon.

'Ah reckon Ah did, suh. But he ain' wuth no trouble.' Jefferson shot Wybourn a contemptuous look.

Hyde sat back again, smoothing down his clothes. Mary couldn't resist speaking.

'I don't mean to be rude, but Jefferson, it was men like Mr Hyde who made their wealth from keeping your people as slaves. Why should you defend him? I don't understand.'

'That's jest exactly so, ma'am,' Jefferson replied solemnly. 'Ah's a Confedrute too. Ah went to the War with my master, an I looked after him, an' 'quired boots fer him when there weren't none. Mist' Boyd, he was shore good to us, an' we was real proud of him. There weren't no one in Blossom County could ride a hoss like Mist' Boyd. We was proud to be his men an' that's somethin' you Yankees ain't never understood.'

Hyde nodded agreement to Jefferson's unusually long speech. 'That life's all gone now,' he said, closing the subject.

Back on the wagon box, Robinson had propped the rifle against his legs and was making rapid shorthand notes. Whiskers Spragg glanced at his inattentive guard, and shook his head.

Uneasy tension smouldered among the passengers for the rest of the day. The halt at Acala was nothing more than a deserted shack a little way off the main trail. There was no corral but Spragg improvised hobbles for the horses. Don cleared some of the bulkier goods from the wagon so he and Mary could sleep in it, while the other men shared the single room of the shack.

While Mary contrived a stew from her own stores, Hyde wandered out to check on his horse and deliberately met up with Cullen.

'We're taking second watch together,' he told the salesman.

'Fine.' Cullen nodded and changed direction slightly to pass the taller man.

Hyde turned, his grey eyes narrowed. 'Cullen. You aiming to find that map tonight?'

Cullen stopped, a cheery smile showing on his face. 'You think I don't want the mine any more?'

Hyde didn't respond to the smile. 'You're not acting same as you were last night. There was sure something on your mind then, but it's different now.'

'Black Dog threw his best at us today and we got the best of the deal. Everyone's less worried than we were last night.' Cullen produced a quick explanation.

Hyde took half a pace closer. 'Why, you're not aiming to run out on me, are you? We made a deal, remember?'

'Of course. I got more sense than to get you mad at me,' he answered honestly. Hyde's attack on Wybourn earlier confirmed Cullen's impression that the Southerner would be a very bad man to cross. Cullen was pretty confident about handling his own affairs, but he knew he lacked real gun skill.

'Then you'll be searching for that map tonight?' Hyde asked.

'Sure.' Cullen just had to hope that he didn't disturb Wybourn. Or that Hyde would help defend him from the businessman's wrath if he did.

When he got back to the adobe, Cullen found he had little appetite for Mary's good stew. He picked at it, thinking mostly about the dilemma he had got caught in. Mary Schmidt thought his bruised ribs were hurting him as he ate, and piled extra food on to his tin plate in sympathy.

During his watch, Cullen made a show of searching Wybourn's valise, and found precisely nothing.

'I reckon maybe you were right,' he told Hyde quietly. 'Perhaps Wybourn does keep it locked up someplace in El Paso.'

'Then we'll search for it there,' Hyde said, watching the salesman in the dim light.

'Oh, I'll get that map one way or the other,' Cullen answered.

'Good.' Hyde didn't want to say more. All the things that he had lost in the War he could never regain. His family plantation had been sold to carpetbaggers and the unthinking, easy life, cushioned by wealth and status, was lost. He knew he could never recapture that past, but Cullen's silver mine offered a real chance to get back some of the money. For the rest of the silent watch, the Southerner made plans for finding the map, wherever it was, and making the mine work.

The night passed uneventfully and the travellers were in a cheerful mood the next morning.

'Get on up there, my beauties, an' we'll be in El Paso by noon,' Whiskers Spragg called, swinging his whip over the team. The horses trotted out at a good pace. The expert attentions of Spragg and Jefferson, with liberal helpings of the grain the stage was supposed to be delivering, had kept them in good condition.

'It's a swell morning, yeah?' Robinson said from his place on the box beside the driver. He had made the effort to tidy up that morning. His dark curls had been successfully smoothed down with patent hair oil but his shaving had been rather hit and miss without the benefit of a mirror. 'I shall be rather sorry to arrive in a town and take my leave of you-all, but I already have a great deal to put in my next letter back to the editor.'

'El Paso ain't all that civilized.' A stream of tobacco juice hit a clump of grass.

'A hot bath wouldn't go amiss,' Robinson said thoughtfully. 'Nor would a bed with a mattress.'

Spragg chuckled to himself.

Inside the wagon, Mary was singing gently to herself. The men listened peacefully, enjoying her sweet soprano voice. Only her husband couldn't hear, as he was riding Hyde's liver chestnut horse again. Hyde was feeling better in himself after his peaceful night, and his arm didn't ache, but the slight injury made a good excuse for him to ride on the wagon. He wasn't about to let either Wybourn or Cullen out of his sight if he could help it.

Cullen was restless. He sat casually on his usual seat, leaning against the sacks of mail, but his bright blue eyes kept flickering back and forth. They would settle on Wybourn for a while, then dart about. Cullen drew his pocket-watch from his waistcoat and studied it, even though they had been travelling barely half an hour. By noon, they would be in El Paso. At noon, Wybourn would hand over to him the map he had been seeking for four years. Cullen resisted the urge to look at his pocket-watch yet again. Even the occasional stab of pain from his ribs didn't bother him too much. He was more concerned over whether Wybourn would keep his word. Cullen found he was clenching his fists, and forced himself to relax.

Only Hyde noticed the tell-tale signs of agitation. He waited patiently, ready to take a hand in whatever developed.

Whiskers Spragg was restless too, but his was an eagerness to get the stage in as quickly as possible.

'I ain't been late in more'n two years,' he complained.

'You can't be held to blame if there are Comanches on the war-trail, yeah?' Robinson did his best to be consoling.

Spragg turned to him, blue eyes blazing from his leathery, whiskery face. 'I ain't let nothin' stop me afore. Injuns, *bandidos*, storms, blizzards. Nothin'. Whiskers Spragg allus gets the stage through plumb on time.'

'I bet the storms out here aren't so bad as they are back East,' Robinson said with a cunning that didn't show in his open, honest face.

He wasn't disappointed. The old-timer glared at him as if he were a particularly persistent tax official.

'I reckons you cain't set yer clocks by the weather back East,' Spragg started. 'Out on the plains, you could bet yer favourite hoss it's gonna storm at four o'clock. And it ain't no summer shower either. Why, I've seen lightnin' kill a hundred buffalo at one time. Jest the one bolt too.'

Having got Spragg started, Robinson started to search his jacket pocket for his notebook. Then he realized that he'd have to put the rifle down to write notes. The danger of an Indian attack was surely much less, but there seemed to be an endless supply of other dangerous types out here. Instead he just listened, committing Spragg's stories to memory

The easy mood was all too abruptly shattered when the stage rounded a corner of the trail and found the remains of a tragedy waiting there. A cloud of turkey buzzards flapped into the blue sky, calling harshly to each other.

'Oh my,' said Robinson.

'Hell's teeth,' said Spragg, sadly.

9

A buckboard was standing in the middle of the trail. One horse lay dead in its harness; the other was missing. A man's body lay by the side of the buckboard and a woman was slumped on the seat.

'Whoa there now!' Spragg drew his team to a halt.

The horses stood blowing, their ears all pointing to the strange thing ahead of them. Robinson raised the Winchester and looked around for any sign of Indians, even before taking a good look at the buckboard. Behind him, the other passengers were drawing guns and shifting to try and see the cause of concern. Don Schmidt halted the horse next to the wagon. The liver chestnut suddenly put its head down to rub its knee, and nearly pulled him from the saddle.

'I don't reckon as there's any danger now,' Spragg said.

Hauling the wagon's brakes on, he jumped down. Robinson followed, still keeping the rifle ready for use.

'How can you tell?' he asked quietly. The light wind shifted and he wrinkled his nose in disgust. 'What in heaven is that dreadful smell?'

'Bodies rottin' in the sun,' Spragg answered bluntly.

Robinson stopped, suddenly feeling sick as his vivid imagination pictured what might be ahead. Then he made himself go on and take his share in seeing what could be done.

'The Comanches must've bushwhacked 'em a couple of days back,' Spragg concluded when they'd examined the remains.

Wybourn and Hyde agreed with him. Cullen had said very little through the whole sorry business. He stood slightly aside from the others, picking at a bullet hole in the side of the buckboard. The wood was liberally peppered with bullet marks, and a couple of shots had brought down the dead horse. Both bodies had been mutilated in a way which showed this had been a Comanche attack, not *bandidos*. Repeating rifles had given the Comanches the ability to carry out this attack. The man had been shot once and then probably hit with a hatchet. His wife had been shot at very close range, by a larger gun. There was no gun to be seen, but the farmer still wore a gun belt with a holster for a large Colt, like Spragg's Dragoon.

'Most likely shot her so's the Comanches couldn't get their goddamn hands on her,' Spragg said.

'Would he really do that?' Robinson asked. His dark eyes were troubled by what they had seen. 'Don't Indians sometimes take captives and then trade them for gifts?'

'Sometimes,' Spragg agreed. 'An' sometimes they jest rapes an' kills 'em.'

'What can we do now?' Robinson

wanted to be active, to be doing something so he didn't have time to stop and think too hard about this horror. For once, he wasn't framing what he had seen into a letter.

'Give the poor souls a decent Christian burial,' Wybourn said. He had found a rolled tarp in the back of the buckboard, and he laid it gently over the woman's body.

Cullen started, and looked at him with sheer disbelief. The other men were too busy talking to notice the raw anger that flickered across Cullen's round face.

'We ain't got the time,' Spragg objected. 'This stage is runnin' late anyhow,' he added, spitting tobacco at the buckboard wheel and missing.

'We can't leave them any longer for the coyotes and buzzards to pick at.'

'We kin burn 'em, buckboard an' all.'

'We'd surely better take something to identify them with,' Hyde drawled. 'The sheriff can find any relatives.'

'All right.'

The bodies were laid together in the back of the buckboard. Hyde found a letter that the woman had written and must have intended to post when she reached town. The men unhitched the dead horse and pushed the buckboard off the trail to an open spot on the valley floor, on a sandy patch near the creek. It could burn there without too much danger. Creosote bush was piled in the back and the whole lot set alight. Robinson read a prayer aloud as they watched the fire take hold. Through it all, Cullen remained silent, except for adding an 'amen' at the end of the Lord's Prayer.

The wagon was soon under way again, but the cheer of the morning had gone. Fear of the Comanche had returned, even though the attack on the buckboard had happened before their own defeat of Black Dog and his warriors. A plume of smoke rose into the sky behind them as a reminder of what they had escaped. Hyde was covertly watching Cullen. The earlier restlessness had gone; the salesman was quiet and still, occupied with his own thoughts. He seemed troubled by what he had seen, as they all were, but Hyde suspected there was more to Cullen's mood. He was still glancing at Wybourn, but there was disgust in Cullen's face now. He looked like a man who was keeping an uncomfortable secret.

Robinson was thinking about the incident too. He shifted his long legs around in the wagon box.

'You still feelin' badly about them buck you shot yesterday?' Spragg asked, lazily chewing on his tobacco.

'I don't know.'

'You're sure seein' plenty of that for-real frontier you done come out to write about.'

'I can hardly complain, can I?' Robinson agreed. 'I was hoping for some real excitements, and I got them.'

Spragg flashed a grin from the depths

of his wiry beard. Robinson might have started out as a fancy-speaking greenhorn, but the old-timer liked the way he mucked in and took what came without everlastingly complaining. He thought Robinson had the makings of a real Westerner. 'You'll do,' he said.

Robinson understood this for the high praise it was. Impulsive as ever, he took the moment to ask, 'I tell you what I've a hankering to really do, yeah? I should admire, just briefly, to drive a six-horse team like yours. I never drove more than two horses before, yeah, and they were only farm horses.'

'These are my team,' Spragg said defensively.

'Sure. But on a flat trail and wide stretch like this, I surely couldn't go far wrong? I couldn't get as skilled as you are,' he added with honest flattery. 'But you could help me get the feel of it. You never know how tricky a thing is until you've tried it for yourself,' he said cunningly.

Robinson had his full attention on Spragg as he pleaded his case. He vaguely noticed the cloud of white winged doves bursting from an overgrown arroyo ahead, but it didn't register. Spragg understood what was happening even before the Comanches launched their ambush.

'Yeeaahh!' he screamed, shaking the reins.

Half a dozen Comanches burst into view, galloping hell for leather towards the wagon. Spragg leaned forward and urged his team right towards them.

For this attack Black Dog was in the lead. His tall sorrel paint raced ahead of the other mounts, closing the distance to the wagon with raking strides. This time, the war leader was dressed in his best. Half a dozen eagle feathers fluttered from the ends of his long, fur-wrapped braids. The upper half of his face was painted yellow and the lower part was black, like the stripes along his powerful arms. His rifle had been left behind; now he carried a seven foot lance in his right hand and a shield fringed with feathers and scalplocks on his left arm. Right behind him came his last five warriors.

Robinson swiftly raised the Winchester to his shoulder, but held his fire. It was partly because he simply wanted to look at the for-real, painted warriors charging towards him, and also because he knew his chances of hitting at longer range were poor, especially from a jolting wagon. His quick mind calculated the risks and he waited for those first moments.

Don Schmidt had been riding towards the rear of the wagon, and was taken by surprise when it jerked forward into a run. Tightening his left-handed hold on the reins, he booted Hyde's liver chestnut in the ribs. The horse plunged into a gallop, tossing its head to try and escape the pressure on the reins. Don was pulled forward in the deep saddle, his position made awkward by the shotgun he was carrying under his right arm.

'Stop it,' he insisted, pulling on the reins to try and calm the horse. Don had always ridden farm horses with mild, snaffle bits; he hadn't realized that Hyde's mount had a curb bit which produced greater control, or greater pain if misused. Unsure of himself, he tried to hang on by clinging to the reins.

The maddened horse fought him, curvetting round and humping its back. Clinging uncomfortably to the saddle horn, Don spared a moment to look up, and saw he was getting left behind.

'Oh, get on with you!' Don released his tight hold and kicked the horse again.

Frightened and confused, it snatched the bit and bolted into a gallop. Don clung on for dear life as the liver chestnut thundered up to and then past the wagon.

'Stop! Whoa!' He tried hauling on the reins again, but the horse had the bit between its teeth, and he had no effect.

Whoops and shrieks abruptly reminded Don of a more pressing danger. The Comanches were only fifty yards away and getting closer every second. Abandoning any attempt to control his bolting mount, he wrapped the reins around the saddle horn and lifted the shotgun to his shoulder.

'Look at that for courage!' Robinson exclaimed as Don raced alongside the six-horse team.

The other passengers were in almost as much confusion. As Spragg gave his ringing cry, Cullen sat up suddenly, swore and fell back, clutching his side.

'Let me by,' ordered Hyde. He was climbing to the front of the wagon and trying to see out.

Mary Schmidt snatched up Cullen's short-barrelled revolver, which he had been keeping close by. He was too slow to stop her, hampered by the throbbing pain in his ribs. She unfastened a canvas curtain on the left of the wagon and peered out.

Wilbur Jefferson stayed at the rear.

He muttered a prayer to himself and lifted the long axe. Beside him, Wybourn readied his revolver.

'There ain't but five of them,' Hyde reported. He got one knee on the front bench and braced himself to aim.

'They're still not using their rifles,' Mary added.

She wouldn't have been so confident if she had been able to see her husband. Don Schmidt had passed the right side of the wagon and was on the off side of the galloping team. The Comanches were racing towards them from the left. Don could see the warriors getting closer all the time. Stuck on a bolting horse, he started shooting before the Comanches could get close enough to it with their lances and clubs. The first blast from the shotgun went past Black Dog, who whooped and slipped sideways from his horse.

'I got him!' Don yelled, cocking the other trigger.

The others knew better. Black Dog was hanging from a loop of rope braided into his horse's mane. He hung alongside his racing mount, one foot over its spine, and his weapons ready in his hands. He was just as dangerous as before, but harder to hit.

Robinson opened fire, aiming for the mass of Comanches behind their leader. The rifle's lever action was stiffer than he had thought, but he kept the stock well braced into his shoulder.

The first couple of shots had no effect, but then he saw one of the Indians reel and clutch his pony's mane. This time Robinson didn't whoop or draw attention to his success. He flicked the lever through the loading cycle and started to aim again.

Don wasn't thinking so carefully. He swung the shotgun in the general direction of the Comanches and let off the other barrel. But in his excitement, and galloping at speed, the shotgun was pointing in the wrong direction. The full load of shot went into the head and neck of the nearest team horse.

The chestnut mare screamed and fell, throwing the rest of the team into confusion. Spragg was as surprised as anyone.

'Whoa! Hold up there!' he called instinctively, gathering up the reins.

The lead horses were still trying to gallop. The wheelers both skidded to a halt, their hooves tearing into the earth. The gelding harnessed to the dying mare went to his knees as the sudden weight dragged at him. He threw his head up, squealing in protest, as he scrambled back to his feet. The wagon was effectively out of control, in danger of running on to the already frightened horses.

Robinson dropped the Winchester and grabbed for the wagon's brake with both hands. He hauled on it frantically as the wagon bounced and slewed, coming to an abrupt halt. He bumped around on the box, but his firm grip on the brake kept him there.

Spragg wasn't so lucky. With no secure hold, he was thrown clear from the box. He bounced against the rump of a horse and landed on his back, gasping for breath.

Inside, Hyde was thrown forward, landing on Cullen. Mary was nearly catapulted over the side, only saving herself by a frantic grab at a pole. Wybourn was tipped into a heap between the benches and banged his head hard against the wagon box. Jefferson managed to grab the tail-gate but bit his tongue as the wagon juddered to a halt.

'Hellfire!'

Hyde picked himself up, trying not to hurt Cullen any more in the process. He sprang on to the box, a gun in each hand. Below him Cullen was gasping painfully. Each breath drove jabs of pain into his cracked ribs and sent pains through his side. Beads of sweat rolled down his face. He urgently wanted to find out what was happening, and help if possible, but he was in too much pain to do anything for the moment. Nearby, Mary could hear his painful breathing, but she didn't dare do anything other than call to him.

'Mr Cullen? Pat? Do you need me?' She clasped his gun firmly in her right hand and used the left to pull back the hammer.

'No . . . No.'

Holding the gun two-handed, Mary fired at the Comanches. The gun kicked back harder than she expected, preventing her from seeing if she hit one or not. Doggedly, she thumbed back the hammer and aimed again.

The Comanches whooped with excitement as the wagon came to its uncontrolled halt. Black Dog swung himself astride his horse again and brandished his lance in the air. These white-eyes had spoiled his medicine and killed many of his most loyal followers. This attack was a do-or-die mission to regain his lost prestige.

The Comanche warrior steered his horse with his knees, aiming the tall paint towards the man on the ground.

He had to switch the lance to his left side, as Spragg was so close to the team.

Even though he was winded, the old-timer forced himself into action. Rolling, he groped for the Dragoon even as he was getting to his knees. The heavy old gun was still in its holster. Spragg heard the thundering hooves, glimpsed the lance being lowered towards him. He threw himself backward, firing the gun blindly. The lance-tip tore fringing from his buckskin shirt. A horse screamed. Spragg landed almost under the hooves of his team. The bay gelding snorted, its ears pinned back with fear, and lashed out. Its hoof caught the old-timer's shoulder with a glancing blow.

'Goddamn it!' Spragg spat his chunk of tobacco out as he rolled away and tried to see what had happened to the warrior.

The awkward angle made Black Dog miss his target. His war horse screamed as the Dragoon's round bullet ripped through its ribs. Acting instantly, Black Dog slipped the loop of rope off and stepped clear of his horse as it fell under him. The paint almost crashed into the stationary wagon and lay kicking, squealing in agony as its blood soaked into the torn grass. Years of training allowed Black Dog to land on his feet and under control. He spun around, doubling back to count coup on the man who had killed his favourite horse, a crime akin to murder by Comanche standards. Spragg was rolling away from the frightened, stamping team horses. Ignoring the gunfire all around them, Black Dog stooped for a moment to remove his moccasins. It was a sign that he wasn't going to retreat from this fight. With his courage made clear, Black Dog dashed in to fight at close quarters.

The other Comanches rode wide, circling the wagon in a loose group. Hyde got off a couple of shots, while Robinson ducked to pick up the Winchester he had dropped. One of the horses squealed and stumbled but its rider forced it on. Then Black Dog was crashing past right by the front wheels of the wagon. The other Indians were out of sight, hidden by the body of the wagon as they circled it. Mary fired, forcing them to keep their distance a little longer. Wybourn had stunned himself when the wagon crashed to a stop, and was still blinking at the canvas roof. He knew vaguely that he would be all right in a few minutes, but the time might not be spared to them.

'What the hell?'

Black Dog's injured horse lay kicking and screaming almost under the wagon. Hyde moved and peered over the edge of the box. A quick glance told him the situation was hopeless. The paint horse was no threat, but Hyde took a moment to send a bullet into its head and end its agony. Then Robinson started firing behind him as the Comanches came into view on the right.

The newspaperman knew he wasn't hitting much, even though now the wagon wasn't moving.

'Go away. Just go away,' he muttered, trying to line the end of the barrel on the swiftly moving targets.

Two of the riders had slipped over the sides of their ponies, as Black Dog had done earlier. They didn't keep to any steady formation, but changed speed and position as their wiry ponies galloped over the rough ground. The Comanches rode their horses as if they had grown on to them, completely at home though none of them used anything more elaborate than a hackamore bridle or a blanket for a saddle pad. The painted ponies, feathers and amulets braided into manes and tails, raced along under complete control. Robinson automatically noticed all the details, even though he didn't have time to think about them. An arrow thudded into the woodwork of the wagon near his leg, but he barely noticed. His first and only priority was to defend the wagon.

Don Schmidt was also astride a galloping horse, but he was a lot less graceful than the Comanches. The bolting liver chestnut carried him past the team horses and away from the fight.

'Stop! Stop! Whoa!'

The shotgun was empty and Don knew he couldn't possibly reload it on a galloping horse. He had to get back in control. He managed to cram the shotgun rather awkwardly into the rifle boot attached to the saddle, and got hold of the reins with both hands. Shoving his feet well home in the wide stirrups, he tugged the reins, released, and tugged sharply again. The liver chestnut threw its head up and down in distress, but the rhythm of its stride started to break.

'Whoa up there. Whoa.' Don managed to sound calm. There was gunfire behind him, and the yells of the Comanches. He couldn't spare time to glance back at the wagon, where Mary was. He concentrated entirely on slowing the horse.

'Whoa there, boy,' he repeated, trying to remember what Hyde called his horse.

Don leaned back in the saddle, taking a firm contact on the reins without actually pulling. The horse began to respond. Encouraged, Don stopped trying to halt it, and instead steered it in a circle. The horse obeyed, settling into a more controlled lope instead of the headstrong gallop. Pointing it at the wagon, Don set off back to the fight, with absolutely no idea of what he was going to do when he got there.

Whiskers Spragg had just about got to his feet as Black Dog came charging in. The Comanche chief thrust underarm, the tip of the lance aiming for the driver's belly. Spragg twisted frantically, feeling the lance snag on his buckskin shirt as it scraped past. Black Dog kept going, swinging his shield up to slam into the other man. Spragg didn't have enough time to respond. The stocky Comanche rammed into the old-timer, knocking the lighter man clear off his feet. Spragg tried to twist as he fell, but he no longer had the agility of his younger days. He landed heavily, losing his Colt as it was jarred from his grip. Black Dog whirled round, lifting and swinging the lance to attack again.

Spragg was gasping but not helpless. He lay still for a few vital moments, as Black Dog charged, recovering his strength. The lance tip flashed down. Spragg writhed, deflecting the lance with his arm while kicking out. His hard, moccasinned foot slammed into the side of the Comanche's knee, taking him off balance just as the lance pierced the ground beside Spragg's shoulder.

Black Dog staggered, catching the lance-tip on the ground. He screamed defiance as he wrenched it clear again, fighting to regain his balance. It gave Spragg the time he needed. The Colt Dragoon was too far away to help. The old-timer scrambled up while drawing the skinning knife from its sheath.

As Black Dog turned back, Spragg was advancing to meet him. The wiry old-timer dashed forward, aiming to get inside the reach of the seven-foot lance. But Black Dog had the reflexes of a trained warrior in his prime. He took a long step back and thrust the lance upwards. It was a move that could disembowel a man with one stroke.

10

Hyde knew he only had a few rounds left in his revolvers. He crouched on the box and picked off careful shots at the circling Comanches. He brought down one horse, its rider landing gracefully on his feet. Another Comanche whirled his mount around, intending to pick up his dismounted friend, but the warrior left the circle and sped across the open ground to the wagon. His mounted friends backed him up. With whoops and shrieks they charged the wagon. Both Robinson and Hyde ducked from the hail of arrows and gunfire.

'Jesus!' Robinson exclaimed. He glanced across at the other man. 'What can we do?' Excitement coloured his voice but he showed no signs of panic. A bullet tore splinters from the frame of the wagon just above his head. Robinson ducked, but didn't even look.

'We keep fighting,' Hyde answered. He spared a brief glance for the fight between Spragg and Black Dog, which was happening a few feet away, but he didn't have time to help. Using the front of the box as cover, he took a careful shot.

The running brave stumbled to his knees, but picked himself up. Blood was pouring thickly down his side, but he lifted his club and came on. The other braves split to attack the wagon from different sides. One pair raced to the rear. With the canvas curtains down, they couldn't see what was happening inside the wagon. The younger brave kneed his mount right to the tail-gate, aiming to leap inside. As the pony skidded to a halt, Jefferson rose into view. The long-handled axe swung round and bit into the brave's side as he made the jump. The Comanche screamed in agony and fell between the wagon and the frightened pony, which backed away.

'Yuh ain't goin' to hurt no more

folks!' Jefferson yelled. He leaped from the safety of the wagon, landing almost on top of the injured brave. The Comanche had never seen a black man before and stared at him in astonishment as Jefferson lifted the axe overhead for a killing blow. The brave was too slow in reacting. The axe blade sliced into his chest, opening heart and lungs. There was a wet, gargling scream, silenced when Jefferson struck again.

The second warrior was more cautious. Bringing his horse round in a sharp turn, he drew back his bow and aimed at the strange brown-skinned man.

Back in the wagon, Mary had clambered over the benches to the back. Ignoring Wybourn, who was carefully getting up again and mopping blood from his scalp, she saw Jefferson jump out after the injured Comanche.

'Be careful!' she exclaimed, her words almost drowned under the man's dying screams. She hurriedly looked away, then saw the second Comanche aiming his bow and arrow.

'Look out!' she screamed, raising Cullen's gun two-handed.

Jefferson acted instantly. He flung himself sideways, using the loose pony for cover. An arrow hit the tail-gate of the wagon just as Mary fired. She was astonished to see her target jerk and almost drop his weapons.

'Yuh stay there, ma'am,' Jefferson snapped.

Grabbing the pony's mane, he swung himself astride with the assurance of one who has snatched many bareback rides to and from the fields. Kneeing the startled pony around, he raced it towards the injured Comanche, the axe still in his hands. Mary suddenly remembered to cock the gun again, but Jefferson was in her line of sight.

'I'll take care of it,' Wybourn said, drawing his Navy Colt.

'Never mind,' Mary exclaimed impatiently. 'We can manage.'

Out on the wagon box, Hyde and Robinson were being kept busy. Two mounted warriors were racing to the attack, both hanging alongside their horses. Hyde fired two shots and heard the hammer click on an empty chamber. He dropped the gun and switched the one in his left hand across. Robinson balanced the rifle barrel on the front of the box and blasted off shots as fast as he could manage. A horse ploughed into the ground, kicking and thrashing. The other rider hauled his pony around in a tight turn and raced to his friend's help. The first brave scrambled to his feet and vaulted on to the galloping pony. Behind them was the Comanche whose pony had been shot down earlier. He swerved past them and charged for the wagon in a suicidal rush. A blast of bullets met him, knocking him clear off his feet before he could get close. His gesture bought the other two enough time to get firmly astride the burdened pony. Hyde had run out of bullets. He was a little shaky and his injured arm was throbbing, but it didn't seem to be bleeding. He crouched in the bottom of the driver's box and started reloading. Robinson fired another shot after the fleeing Indians, but the flush of urgency had left him. The rifle kicked painfully against his shoulder, warning him that a splendid bruise was developing. He loaded another bullet into the chamber, but held his fire. The two Comanches in his sights fled without looking back.

Jefferson screamed at the top of his voice as he charged the injured Comanche. The trained war pony obeyed knee-pressure commands as its rider swung his axe in the air. His target lost his nerve. The Comanche swooped sideways to grab up his dropped bow from the ground, and sent his pony into a sprint. The brave made no attempt to use the weapon, but crouched over the pony's neck, urging it on. Jefferson gave chase, lowering the axe so he could cling to his pony's mane with one hand as it bounded over the rough ground.

'Jefferson!' Mary yelled. 'Come back! Jefferson!'

A lifetime of obedience to commands penetrated his excitement. Jefferson leaned back, slowing the pony and bringing it round. Looking around, he could see a double-mounted pair fleeing to the woods on the other side of the creek. A glance reassured him that the one ahead was also intent on escape. The black man sat boldly on the war pony, the bloody axe across his knees.

'We shore showed them Injuns,' he said to himself, a broad grin spreading across his face. 'Ah reckons I kin do mighty well out here.' Turning the pony, he urged it back to the wagon.

Black Dog grunted his coup cry as his lance struck upwards at the leathery wagon driver. Spragg twisted his torso to the left and swung a blocking blow with his right arm. The flat of his skinning knife hit the lance shaft and deflected it just enough. The metal point tore through Spragg's buckskin shirt and the faded undershirt, opening a cut on his side. He kept moving forward, trapping the lance between himself and the Comanche warrior.

Black Dog swung his shield across. Spragg let himself run into it, letting his enemy absorb his momentum. Black Dog couldn't use his lance, as the two men glared into each other's faces, but Spragg's skinning knife was blocked by the shield. The driver knew that a Comanche shield could block bullets from fifty yards, so there was no point in trying to hack through it. He shoved hard against the shield, getting a push back in return. A vivid smile flashed on Black Dog's broad face as they fought; he would certainly win any trial of strength. When the Comanche was occupied in trying to overbear him, Spragg slipped suddenly aside and let fly a kick as the Comanche lurched forward.

His toes caught the warrior right in the groin. Tough as he was, even Black Dog couldn't help a cry of pain as he staggered momentarily. Spragg switched the knife from hand to hand and lunged in. The long blade of the skinning knife went under the edge of the shield and sliced deep. Black Dog screamed as he twisted himself away. He swung his shield up, getting a glancing blow on Spragg's right shoulder. The wagon driver grunted and attacked again. He recklessly dived at the Comanche, stabbing the knife in brutally. It tore up under Black Dog's ribs, bringing a spurt of scarlet blood with it. The warrior reeled back, coughing blood.

'You done made me late,' Spragg hissed. 'I ain't never brought the stage in late afore.'

Even though the warrior was wounded, Spragg knew he was still dangerous. The old-timer feinted to the right and attacked again. Black Dog tried to shield-slam again, but his reflexes were slowing. Spragg got in a third hit, this time between the ribs.

Black Dog staggered back a couple

of paces and fell. More blood gushed from his mouth and nose, smearing the black-and-yellow war-paint. He was struggling to breathe and kept trying to lift his head. Spragg bent and picked up the fallen lance. With a single thrust he pinned it through the Comanche's throat. Black Dog convulsed and slowly relaxed into death. His blood soaked steadily into the grass.

'Are you all right?' Robinson leaned over the driver's box to see what was happening below. 'Oh my.'

'He ain't gonna raid no more places,' Spragg said with satisfaction. Pinning the corpse down with one foot, he wrenched the lance out again.

'I imagine not,' Robinson answered dryly.

Don Schmidt came cantering back on the liver chestnut, rather ashamed. 'Is everyone all right?' he asked anxiously, peering into the wagon.

'I'm fine, dear,' Mary answered, poking her head out. 'Thanks to Mr Jefferson.'

'It shore weren't no trouble,' the black man answered bashfully.

Hyde looked at the long axe balanced over Jefferson's lap and smiled privately.

'What about my hosses!' Spragg bellowed. He sprinted round the team to reach the dead mare. He knelt beside her, stroking her red-brown neck. 'My li'l Rose,' he murmured.

'Oh dear!' Mary exclaimed, discovering for the first time why the wagon had stopped so abruptly. 'What happened?'

'I was trying to hit . . . ' Don started to explain and shut up suddenly. His faint hope, that Spragg might not have heard him, didn't happen. The leathery driver bounded to his feet.

'You shot Rose, you son of a bitch!' His tobacco-stained whiskers quivered with indignation. 'You ain't ridin' no further in this-here wagon, you murderer!'

'I was trying to hit the Comanches,' Don protested.

'An' you got my Rose.'

Spragg's anger was making the other

horses restless. The dead mare's team mate snorted and laid back its ears. Spragg stopped shouting and moved to soothe the frightened gelding.

'Don't you worry none now, Raven,' he told the white horse. Giving the horse another pat, he started to unharness the dead mare.

'Lemme help,' Jefferson offered.

While the two men dealt with the team, the other passengers sorted themselves out. Robinson helped Hyde and Cullen move the Indians' bodies away.

'Do they bury their dead?' he asked, dropping Black Dog's bloody remains into an arroyo.

'I believe so,' Hyde answered carelessly.

'Then shouldn't we cover them with some earth at least, yeah?'

'You can if you wish, but I'm sure not going to bother.' Hyde stood and eased his back. 'Why cheat the buzzards out of a good meal?'

'Or a bad one,' Cullen said sharply.

'He was a man like us,' Robinson said, kicking some loose dirt on to the body.

Crumpled and still, Black Dog looked like just an ordinary man, in spite of the smeared war-paint and buckskin clothes.

'He had dignity and pride too. He was fighting for what he believed in,' Robinson insisted.

Cullen also pushed dirt into the arroyo, half-covering the dead man's face. He had no regret at knowing Black Dog was dead, but he wished the warrior had never taken his bucks on the war-path. Cullen knew in his heart that Black Dog was the sort to go down fighting anyway, but the presence of the repeating rifles had made the raids bolder and more vicious.

'He also did his best to kill me; twice,' Hyde said before walking away.

Robinson looked at the dead man a moment longer, then went to wash his hands in the creek. Cullen trailed silently behind.

Back at the wagon, Don Schmidt had gathered up the Indians' abandoned weapons.

'We can't leave those for *bandidos* or other bad-hat bucks to find,' Wybourn said. The small cut on his temple had dried but a bruise was forming around it. Even with the trickle of dried blood on his face, he was still a dignified man.

'Could I keep this?' Don held up one of the new Winchesters. It had brass tacks nailed into a pattern on the stock, but was otherwise in near-perfect condition. 'It wouldn't be stealing, would it?'

'Spoils of war.'

'Good.' Don's attention wandered to the lance and shield. He picked them up, feeling the weight. 'Don't you think these would look swell on the wall of our new place?'

'Maybe. You'd best ask your wife; she might not like them.'

'Right.' Don handed his prizes up to Wybourn for safekeeping, and went to see what was being done about getting the wagon moving again.

The bay pony that Jefferson had taken carried a US Army brand.

'Iffen it ain't learnt to pull harness afore, it can start now,' Spragg decided. He fetched the inevitable wad of black tobacco from his pouch and cut off a chunk. This he offered to the bay. It sniffed suspiciously, then took the offering and chewed it with evident pleasure. With the pony's attention on the strange flavour, Spragg and Jefferson carefully drew on the harness and adjusted it. The bay rolled its eyes and shifted uneasily at the strange touch of full harness, but they got it hitched to the rest of the team without trouble.

'Now we's kin get goin' agin,' Spragg declared confidently. 'All aboard that's comin'!' he bellowed.

The passengers hastily arranged themselves back on the wagon as Spragg cracked his whip in the air. His five team horses threw themselves into the harness, eager to be away from the place that smelled of blood. The new horse snorted and tried to back up, but the other horses pushed it on. Spragg dexterously touched its ears with his whip, startling it into moving without actually hurting.

'Go on there,' he called, his hand firm on the reins. 'Let's be gettin' to business. We got places to go.'

The wagon rolled forward, leaving behind a dead horse and churned-up, blood-soaked ground.

Mary was singing to herself again. She unbraided her dark hair and combed it out.

'Goodness, I must look a mess,' she exclaimed, peering through her dark locks at Cullen.

The dainty flirt fell dead: his thoughts were entirely elsewhere. Mary pursed her pretty rosebud mouth at him, then went on singing as she neatly wound her hair into a coil around her head.

Cullen's attention was on the rifle stowed on the seat next to Mary;

it was one of those taken from the Comanches. In spite of dust, the dark wood still carried its factory polish. The Winchester was newer than any of the guns belonging to the travellers, just like the other captured repeaters. Cullen reminded himself firmly that his mother and sisters deserved to live comfortably. It was only right and proper that the silver his father had found should be used to keep his family, so the women didn't have to work and they could have the same nice things that other folks had. But his conscience couldn't forget the mutilated bodies of the farmer and his wife in the buckboard wagon. And the old-timer at the stage halt. Even those brave, reckless, dangerous Comanches who had taken this last chance to fight for their old ways. Cullen knew, deep in his heart, that his mother wouldn't want to buy her own comfort at the expense of others' lives.

Without explaining himself, Pat Cullen levered off one of his long boots and reached inside. Hyde instantly guessed that something was up. He sat still, one hand resting casually on his gun butt. Cullen withdrew a sheet of paper and unfolded it.

'Wybourn,' he said clearly.

Mary's quiet singing stopped.

'When we get to El Paso, I'm going to the sheriff with this receipt of yours for thirty repeating rifles,' Cullen said. 'Thirty Winchester repeating rifles.'

There was a moment of silence until the implication sank in.

'Goddamn it!' Spragg shoved the team's reins into Robinson's hands and climbed over the back of the box into the wagon. Robinson suddenly found himself driving the six-horse team, but was more interested in what was happening behind him.

'You goddamn bastard!' Whiskers Spragg yelled, scrambling past the others to Wybourn.

'I haven't done anything,' Wybourn insisted, starting to rise.

While the businessman was thinking

about the furious old-timer, Hyde saw his chance to act. He seized Wybourn's right arm and kicked his feet out from under him. Mary squealed and slid rapidly off her bench as Wybourn almost fell on top of her.

'Let me go!' Wybourn yelled.

Spragg struck him heavily across the face. 'You lowdown, sinnin' bastard!' He spat tobacco juice in Wybourn's eyes. 'You sold rifles to them Comanche!'

'I didn't!' Wybourn rubbed his face against his sleeve. With Hyde holding one arm and Spragg hanging on to the other, he could barely move. 'There's no proof.'

'Why, what else did you do with them?' Hyde drawled. His grey eyes glittered coldly.

'I bought them for the bank, for the guards.' Wybourn wasn't looking at the men who were accusing him. He was gazing steadily at Cullen, who was watching in miserable, steady silence.

'Thirty rifles? For that li'l bank?' Spragg said scornfully

'What did you do with the rest then?' Hyde demanded. He started twisting Wybourn's arm against the movement of the joint. Wybourn gasped and gritted his teeth, trying to twist his shoulder and ease the pain.

'I don't believe you,' Hyde said. 'What does a businessman want with thirty repeating rifles?'

'I never sold any to the Comanches,' Wybourn insisted.

Hyde increased the pressure on the trapped arm.

'Stop it!' Mary cried suddenly. The men looked at her. She coloured, but went on. 'You haven't any proof he gave his rifles to the Indians, and he says he didn't. A man is innocent until proven guilty, isn't he?'

'That's the only reason why this skunk ain't decoratin' a cottonwood right now,' Spragg growled.

'It doesn't give you the right to hurt him,' Mary said.

'Mrs Schmidt is quite right,' Robinson called. He was twisted awkwardly around on the *box, letting the team make their own pace along the trail. 'If Wybourn is innocent of your charges, yeah, he could sue you in the courts.'

'And if he's guilty, the judge'll hang him just as surely as I want to,' Hyde answered.

'We'll hog-tie the evil cuss an' hand him over to the law in El Paso,' Spragg said. 'You'd best keep that receipt safe,' he added to Cullen.

'I will,' the salesman said quietly.

The simple answer occupied Hyde's thoughts as he helped Spragg deal with Wybourn. They soon had the businessman bound, and his gun belt slung over the wagon box by Spragg's side. Wybourn didn't struggle and only spoke once. He glared at Cullen and said. 'You'll regret that.'

Cullen held his head high. 'I won't.'

Hyde watched with silent sympathy as Cullen turned his back on Wybourn and his past, and set his face to the trail ahead of the wagon, and the arrival in El Paso.

11

Robinson sat proudly on the driver's box as the wagon rolled into El Paso. News of their late arrival went ahead of them, sending a wave of excitement through the frontier town.

'They made it. Whiskers Spragg got 'en through.'

Robinson beamed at the passers-by watching them, and made a futile attempt to flatten his unruly curls.

'How's it feel to be making the news, instead of jest writin' about it, son?' Spragg asked. The old-timer acted calm enough, but the newspaperman could see the gleam of excitement in his blue eyes.

'It's swell,' Robinson answered, not bothering to hide his own eagerness. 'I've gathered plenty of thrilling material for my letters, yeah?'

'I think I've had quite enough

excitement for a while,' Mary Schmidt put in. She leaned out over the box, eager to see the town that would be her new home.

'Now, Mrs Schmidt,' Robinson said. 'You're not on the trail any more, yeah? You've got to start acting like a lady again.'

'Oh, hang being a lady,' Mary retorted, but she pulled her deep bonnet back into its proper place.

'Let's give the folks a show!' Spragg swung his whip high in the air, sending his team on at a gallop.

The team horses knew this was the end of the journey, and ran eagerly. Buggies and pedestrians scattered from their path as the wagon swerved into the main street. A trail of fine dust hung in the air behind them. Whiskers Spragg drove past the stage-company office at the end of the street and halted his team outside the sheriff's office.

'Whoa there, me beauties,' he called. 'You kin look forward to some good feed an' a rest now.'

The horses pulled up, blowing and snorting. The flighty sorrel mare pawed the ground and whinnied so hard she shook all over. Don Schmidt reined in Hyde's liver chestnut horse, feeling pleased with himself for arriving in town on such a good horse, even if it wasn't his own. The people watching didn't know that. A crowd gathered almost at once as Spragg climbed nimbly down from the box.

'I'm goin' to fetch Sheriff Hardaker fer that skunk we's got,' he told Robinson.

Mary Schmidt and Wilbur Jefferson were scrambling out the back of the canvas-sided wagon. Don dismounted, hugged his pretty wife and kissed her rosebud mouth, right there in public.

'Don, really,' she said, colouring prettily, but pleased by his show of affection.

Jefferson stared curiously at some Mexican loungers, who feigned indifference at the still unusual sight of a black man in El Paso. Only Cullen, Hyde and

Wybourn were left inside the wagon.

The businessman raised his bound hands to smooth back the lock of grey hair that fell over his face.

'Are you going to hand that receipt to the sheriff?' he asked.

Cullen raised his chin slightly. 'Yes.'

'Why, he has to now,' Hyde interrupted. 'The others know, and there's no way of going back.'

'There's always a way,' Wybourn said. 'If you want something badly enough.' He held out his hands; the wrists were bound together with a rawhide thong. 'This is your last chance,' he told Cullen.

'You sold rifles to the Comanches,' Cullen said quietly.

'I never sold them the rifles,' Wybourn insisted. His gaze was locked on the younger man's, his hands held out for release.

'No, you didn't sell the repeaters,' Cullen said. 'You gave them away. You knew that if Black Dog went on the war-path, the army would have to move in and chase them back to the reservation. Then it would be safe for you to open the mine out in Indian country. You used the Comanches just like you use everyone else.'

'And you broke your word to me,' Wybourn snapped. 'You broke the deal, and you won't ever see that map!'

Cullen winced briefly. 'My poppa found the silver without a map. I can do the same.'

Wybourn leaned forward, his lean body tense. 'You need that damn map. Help me get clear and I'll give you a share in the mine.'

'No.'

'That mine will make good hard cash. Enough for both of us.' Wybourn was pleading and demanding. The colour was rising in his face as he tried to make a bargain.

'Those repeaters killed people. I couldn't sleep, knowing I helped the man who killed them.' Cullen was trembling, as angry now as the other man.

'Damn your honour!' Wybourn was almost shouting. 'Think of the money. That's gonna let us both live in comfort. I ain't got time to be prospecting elsewhere. All the money I've raised since the War's gone into setting up that mine. You ain't taking that away from me!'

'It was never yours to start with.' Cullen had no idea how much he looked and sounded like his father at that moment. Wybourn was briefly silenced as Cullen rose and leaned towards the wagon box. 'You're gonna stand trial for selling repeaters to the Comanches, you scum.' Cullen spat out the words. He picked up Wybourn's black gun belt from the box. 'Now get out there.'

'You put that down!' Wybourn exclaimed. He lunged to his feet and was pushed down again by Hyde. 'That's mine!'

Cullen was getting close to losing his own temper. 'You're the thief. I don't take orders from you, Jack Wybourn!'

'Give me that!' Wybourn repeated frantically.

'You're nothing but a cheating, selfish bastard. You stole from my poppa and you lied to me when I wrote you.' Cullen slung the gun belt over his left shoulder, the Colt hanging against his chest. 'I should've pulled the trigger on you back on the trail, an' blamed it on the Comanches. If there was justice in this world, Black Dog's bucks would've had your scalp hanging from their lodge poles.'

'Damn you!' Wybourn retorted. He lunged forward again, grabbing for the gun belt.

Cullen saw the move and reacted instinctively. He yanked out the Navy Colt and fired. At such close range, the .36 bullet ripped clean through Wybourn's chest, throwing him backwards. Cullen cocked the Colt smoothly on the recoil and fired again, and again. Wybourn jerked and shuddered. Blood darkened his dusty suit and spilled over the goods stowed beneath the seats.

Wybourn's staring eyes began to glaze over as he lay sprawled in the back of the stagecoach wagon.

Shouts erupted from outside. The wagon rocked as Spragg and Robinson jumped on to the box and others crowded around the tail-gate. Hyde was quick to react.

'You sure saved my life,' he said to Cullen. 'I guess Wybourn didn't want to surrender,' he added to the faces peering in.

The sheriff pushed his way to the front of the group.

Cullen lowered the Navy Colt. 'He was going for the gun,' he said quietly.

'I heard some shouting,' Robinson put in. He was tall enough to peer right over the sheriff's head.

'Wybourn was mighty mad at Cullen here for talking about that receipt,' Hyde drawled. 'I reckon he aimed to kill for that.'

'Strikes me that three bullets is plenty for one feller,' Sheriff Hardaker remarked. He held out his hand. 'Let me see that receipt ol' Spragg's been hollerin' about.'

Cullen handed it over; Hyde gave the sheriff one of the Winchesters they had recovered.

'Hmmm. That's a pretty smart weapon for a buck to be carrying. You could be right about Jack Wybourn,' the sheriff said.

'Cullen shot in self-defence,' Hyde insisted.

'A duel, yeah? I'll have to write my editor about this!' Robinson was flicking shorthand scribbles into his notebook.

The sheriff nodded, and called to people in the crowd to carry the body away. 'Come into my office.'

★ ★ ★

When the talking was over, Cullen and Hyde stood in the shade on the sidewalk. The sheriff intended looking into Wybourn's affairs, but he had accepted their word that Cullen had killed Wybourn in self-defence. Cullen looked tired as he leaned against the hitching rail, but some of the old sparkle had returned to his blue eyes.

'Thanks for speaking up for me,' he said. 'I lost us both that map.'

'You got Robinson a mighty slick ending to his story. You reckon he'll ever find out about wampus cats?' Hyde grinned briefly, then added. 'Wybourn deserved what he got.'

Cullen closed his eyes briefly. 'Seems strange not to be hunting for him any more.' He opened them again and looked at the gun belt, still slung over his shoulder, though now without the Navy Colt. 'I got this souvenir.'

'Why, you're starting to sound like our Hulton F. Robinson,' Hyde said, flashing his sharklike smile. 'You see him with that arrow, lance and all?'

Cullen chuckled and heaved himself off the hitching rail. 'Let's get a drink; I'm buying.'

'Now it would be right ungentlemanly of me to refuse an offer like that.'

They strolled along the sidewalk together. Cullen slid the black gun belt off his shoulder and looked it over. He missed seeing Mary and Don Schmidt leaving an office building on the other side of the street. Hyde saw them, and saw Wilbur Jefferson with them too. They were all talking eagerly but when Mary noticed the two men, she picked up her long skirts and came running across the street.

'Guess what?' she cried.

Cullen came out of his thoughts and waved to her.

'Guess what?' Mary repeated, halting by the sidewalk. The other two followed. 'We've been to see the lawyer handling Uncle Wilder's estate. It's not a farm at all.'

'We've inherited a stock farm,' Don went on, taking his wife's arm. 'Cattle and horses, with just a few acres down to crops.'

'Is that good?' Hyde asked.

'Horses are much nicer than turnips,' Mary said.

'I've never had much stock,' Don interrupted. His face was alight with excitement and pride. 'So we'd thought we'd best hire ourselves a good man to help out.'

'So we hired Wilbur!' Mary finished.

The black man beamed, showing off his uneven teeth. 'Ah's goin' be a foreman,' he said proudly. 'An' Miss Mary, she done promised me a fine hoss, all to myself.'

'That's swell,' Hyde said.

Cullen was about to add his piece, but his attention was suddenly diverted. He'd been idly fiddling with Wybourn's gun belt when his fingers had found a narrow slit, carefully hidden. Inside, he could feel paper.

'Isn't it good?' Mary dragged him back to the present by tugging his sleeve.

'Yeah.' Cullen forced himself to act normal. 'Call at my hotel afore you leave town an' I'll see about getting you a house-warming present from my samples,' he added with a saucy wink.

As soon as he could, Cullen got himself and Hyde away from the others and into a corner of the nearest saloon. The Southerner went along with the hurried goodbyes, sure something was up.

'You thought of something?' Hyde guessed. His own heartbeat pounded faster than before. Could they make a real stab at finding the mine; at getting a chance to make a go of things?

Hyde's unusual eagerness made Cullen realize that now two men's hopes were bound up in the lost mine. He dithered for a moment before easing the folded paper from the secret pocket in the gun belt. Laying it carefully on the scratched table, he unfolded his find.

'That's why Wybourn panicked when you picked up his gun belt,' Hyde breathed.

A map lay between them, worn fragile from age along the folds and with fragments of dirt caught in it.

'That's Poppa's handwriting,' Cullen said, tracing the names on the map with his finger. 'And that sketch there in the corner, the coiled snake, that's his.'

'And there's the mine,' Hyde whispered, turning his head to peer at the map which was upside down to him. 'We got it!'

Cullen could make no answer. He wiped his hand abruptly across his eyes to smudge away the forming tears.

'I got it back,' he said to the air. 'I got it for us, like you wanted, Poppa.'

'Get yourself a mount and we'll ride out there to take a look. There's a whole passel of things for us to do,' Hyde was busy with his own thoughts.

'Sure. Sure.' And Patrick Cullen Williams stopped thinking of the past and began to plan for the future.

We do hope that you have enjoyed reading this large print book.

Did you know that all of our titles are available for purchase?

We publish a wide range of high quality large print books including:
Romances, Mysteries, Classics
General Fiction
Non Fiction and Westerns

Special interest titles available in large print are:
The Little Oxford Dictionary
Music Book, Song Book
Hymn Book, Service Book

Also available from us courtesy of Oxford University Press:
Young Readers' Dictionary
(large print edition)
Young Readers' Thesaurus
(large print edition)

For further information or a free brochure, please contact us at:
Ulverscroft Large Print Books Ltd.,
The Green, Bradgate Road, Anstey,
Leicester, LE7 7FU, England.
Tel: (00 44) **0116 236 4325**
Fax: (00 44) **0116 234 0205**

TRAIL OF THE CIRCLE STAR

Lee Martin

Finding his cousin, friend, and mentor, Marshal Bob Harrington, hanging dead from a cottonwood tree is a cruel blow for Deputy U.S. Marshal Hank Darringer. He'd like nothing better than to exact a bitter and swift revenge, but as a lawman he knows he must haul the murderers to justice — legally. But seeking justice is tougher than obstructing it in Prospect, Colorado. Hank has to keep one hand on his gun and one eye on his back.

McKINNEY'S REVENGE

Mike Stotter

When ranch-hand Thadius McKinney finds his newly-wedded wife in the arms of his boss, the powerful, land-hungry Aaron Wyatt, something inside him snaps. Two gunblasts later, McKinney is forced to flee into the night with the beef-baron's thugs hot on his trail, baying for his blood. A man cannot run forever, and even when his back-trail is littered with bodies, the fighting isn't over. McKinney decides it is time for Wyatt to pay the Devil.

THE BROTHERS DEATH

Bill Wade

Russ Hartmann was a wandering cowboy who had seen better days. Two riders followed him out of the past: one brought good news, the other brought murder and disaster. When the Brothers Death took a hand, it appeared certain that Hartmann would go under. But a ranching lady coveted his skill with a gun, and he went to work for her. Slowly he dug both Evelyn Cross's Broken C and himself out of trouble — but he kept the undertaker busy in the process.

RHONE

James Gordon White

Former bounty hunter Phil Rhone finds himself in a mess of trouble when he agrees to help Brad Miller to find his abducted wife, Lorna. They team up with Susan Prescott, a blonde beauty seeking the killers of her family. The hunt takes them up into the isolated mountains to a slave labour gold mine, where they confront sadistic Nelson Forbes. The odds are against them, but Susan thirsts for revenge and Miller isn't leaving without his wife . . .